MOUNTAIN JACK PIKE

ROCKY MOUNTAIN KILL

#2

Also by Robert J. Randisi

Angel Eyes

Tracker

Mountain Jack Pike

MOUNTAIN JACK PIKE

ROCKY MOUNTAIN KILL

#2

Robert J. Randisi

SPEAKING VOLUMES, LLC

NAPLES, FLORIDA

2012

Rocky Mountain Kill: #2

ISBN 978-1-61232-593-4

PROLOGUE

The snow crunched beneath Jack Pike's boots as he ran. A big man, he left deep depressions behind him as he fled for his life.

Behind him he could hear the harsh breathing of the grizzly, and he could almost feel the bear's hot breath on the back of his neck, which gave wings to his feet.

In his left hand was his Hawken, which for some reason refused to fire. In his left hand was his Kentucky pistol, which also refused to operate. Running, arms pumping furiously, he wondered why he still carried them if they were useless.

The only weapon he had that would do him any good was his knife, which at the moment was in his right boot. All he had to do was let the bear get close to him so he could use it—but the thought of letting the grizzly get that close was too much for Pike, so he just kept running.

It was cold, and the cold seemed to be going right down his throat and into his lungs, which felt frozen.

Soon, he knew, he'd be able to run no farther, and he'd have to turn and face the grizzly, its slavering jaws, its huge paws, its bestial eyes, its simple urge to kill.

Suddenly, ahead of him, he saw a group of men. They were all armed with rifles. They could help him; they could save him. There were enough of them that, when they all fired, the bear would be able to do nothing but die.

As Pike ran on, getting closer and closer to the men, he saw that they were Blackfoot Indians. Maybe they'd help him, anyway. Maybe he and the Indians could combine forces against a common foe.

He was almost as close to the Indians now as the bear was to him, and the braves—too numerous to count—all raised their rifles together. They were going to help him, he thought, until suddenly he realized that the rifles were not pointing at the bear— they were pointing at him! And the braves were laughing, damn them!

He knew now that death was imminent. The only question was whether it would come from the Indians or from the grizzly.

He was trapped between them, and the choice of how he would die was his.

Only he didn't want to die.

He didn't want to die!

"I don't want to die!"

Pike sat straight up and stared around him. He stared at the sides of his tent without realizing where he was for a moment.

Next to him, Skins McConnell sat up and said, "Jesus, Pike, what is it?"

Pike looked at his friend, and then ran his hand over his face. It came away drenched with sweat, in spite of the fact that it was below freezing outside. He wiped it dry on his shirt and noticed that the hand was shaking. He made a fist and pushed it down at his side.

"Pike?" McConnell said, softer this time, "was it the dream again?"

Pike looked at McConnell and took a deep breath.

"Yeah," he said, finally able to speak, "it was the dream again."

"The same one?"

Pike nodded and said, "Shit, yeah . . . the same damn one."

"The grizzly, the Blackfoot . . . everything?" McConnell asked.

Pike nodded and said, "Yeah, everything . . . everything the same." He ran his hand over his face again and wiped it off on his blanket. This time he flexed the hand open and closed a few times to try to stop the shaking.

"How many nights is that, now?"

"Three," Pike said. "Three nights in a row."

"What do you think it means?"

"I don't know," Pike said. What he thought it might have meant was that he was going mad, only he didn't say that. "I don't know."

He took a deep breath and his breathing was almost back to normal now.

"Look, Skins, I'm sorry—"

"Hell, forget it, man," McConnell said, cutting

7

him off. "I've had my share of nightmares . . ." Not three nights in a row, though, he thought. That was *strange!*

"Go back to sleep. When we get to Clark's Fork Trading Post you'd better get yourself a woman and work out whatever it is that's botherin' you. Nothing like working your frustrations out with a good, pillowy woman."

"Yeah," Pike said. "Yeah, you're right, Skins. That's what I'll do. Go back to sleep."

"Yeah, you too," McConnell said, lying back down on his blanket.

But Pike didn't go back to sleep. He couldn't. He stayed awake the rest of the night, wondering what demons were invading his sleep.

PART ONE

THE DREAM

Chapter One

The trading post at Clark's Fork, Wyoming, had started out small. Ted Clark had built himself a little shack and opened for business, trading with trappers and Indians alike. As the years went by, other people came and other structures were erected around his, and eventually he expanded his own small shack into a good-size trading post, complete with supplies, a bar and—if you were on his list of friends—food.

"Jesus," McConnell said as they rode in, "it looks like a town, now."

Most of the structures were still tents, but Pike could see what McConnell meant. The Clark's Fork Trading Post was now as long as a town block, with structures on either side. Since their last trip there Ted Clark had been named honorary mayor of Clark's Fork.

At the end of the block a livery stable had been established. It looked more like an elongated lean-to that had been built for the horses, and next to it a tent had been set up for the liveryman. As they got closer they could see that there were burlap sides on the lean-to, made so that they could be rolled up and down. At the moment, they were tied in the up position.

They rode up to the "stable" and a man stepped out of the tent. Neither Pike nor McConnell knew him. He was tall, in his forties, and he had a nose that resembled a potato.

"Help ya?"

"Yes," Pike said, "we'd like to put up our animals."

The man looked past them at the five mules they were leading.

"I can put your horses in the stable, but the mules'll have to go out back."

"Out back?"

"Gotta corral there."

"Okay," Pike said, dismounting. McConnell dismounted also and both men moved around to face the liveryman.

"How much?" Pike asked, but before the man could answer, McConnell cut in.

"Pike, why don't you let me handle this? Go over to Ted's and get a drink. Order one for me, too."

"Sure, Skins," Pike said, handing McConnell his horse's reins.

"And get us some food," McConnell said. "Preferably something hot."

"You fellas friends of Ted Clark?"

"That's right," McConnell said.

As Pike as walking away he heard the liveryman say, "Well, in that case I can give you a cheaper . . ."

Pike was out of earshot by now, walking toward

Ted Clark's place. His eyes felt gritty because he hadn't slept after the dream last night. His head was pounding because he was thinking about the dream—he'd been thinking about it all day. He knew that was why McConnell had spared him the task of dickering with the liveryman. Skins McConnell was a good friend and he wanted to help, but there was just no way he could. No one could get inside Pike's head to see what the problem was. He had to do that himself.

Pike entered the trading post and saw Ted Clark standing behind his makeshift bar. With the way his business had grown, Pike knew that Clark could have bought himself a real bar and had it shipped from back east, but Clark always said that his original bar was good enough for him when he first opened, and it would always be good enough for him. Across from it was the counter he did his trading post and general store business from.

There were a couple of trappers at the bar and Clark was pouring them drinks. When he finished he looked up, saw Pike, and smiled.

"Pike! You ol' sonofabitch! Come on over here."

Pike grinned and walked up to the bar. He didn't know the two men at the bar, but he had the feeling that they knew him.

"Jesus, I think you got even bigger," Clark said, reaching across the bar to shake hands.

Clark was no slouch himself when it came to size. He was over six feet, weighed better than two hundred, and he had a barrel chest and huge hands. Not only was he the honorary mayor of the Fork, but he was also its unofficial lawman—and he kept the

13

peace with those hands.

"You look like a grizzly," Clark said, kidding. When he saw the stricken look that came into Pike's eyes he said, "Hey, what's wrong?"

"Nothing . . . I've just got a headache," Pike lied. "How about a drink?"

"Sure, sure," Clark said. "You want something to eat, too?"

"Yeah," Pike said, accepting the whiskey, "for me and Skins McConnell."

"Skins is here, too?" Clark said. "Hey, that's great. Listen, Sky Woman has got some stew on the stove out back. Grab a table and I'll bring it out."

Sky Woman was Clark's Crow wife. The food at Clark's Fork had improved dramatically when Clark married her several years back.

"How is Sky Woman?" Pike asked.

"She's great, and her stew's better than ever. Let me go and get it."

"Thanks—and bring another drink, huh? For me, and one for Skins."

"Sure, you bet. Just set yourself down and I'll take care of you."

"Thanks, Ted."

Pike went over and sat down at one of the tables that Clark had built himself. He sipped the whiskey slowly, although he wanted to knock it back and take another right after it. Getting drunk wouldn't help him, though. It wouldn't get rid of his headache, or the grittiness in his eyes, and it certainly wouldn't get rid of the dream.

As Skins McConnell came through the door, Ted Clark came out of the back. He was carrying a tray with two bowls of stew and two drinks.

"Hey, McConnell!" he shouted. "You got your skinny ass here just in time. Sit down!"

"How are you, Ted?" McConnell asked. He approached the table, shook hands with Clark, and sat opposite Pike. "How's Sky Woman?"

"She's fine. She'll say hello later. Go ahead, boys. Eat hearty. Let me know if you want some more drinks."

"How about some beer?" Pike asked.

"Comin' up."

After Clark walked away McConnell said, "How are you doing?"

"I could use some sleep," Pike said. "Otherwise I'm okay."

"We can hole up here for a while, if you want. You could get some sleep."

"Naw," Pike said, "just overnight, I think. Whiskey Sam and Dick Post ought to be here by then. There may be a lot of buffalo out there, but there's also a lot of hunters. Come on, let's eat."

They wolfed down the delicious stew, and when Clark had a chance he came over and sat with them.

"What brings you through this way?"

"Just some buffalo hunting," McConnell said.

"Plenty of them around," Clark said. "Lots of hunters, too."

Pike grinned at McConnell, as if he'd been vindicated.

"This place has grown some since the last time we were here, Ted."

"Sure has," Clark said. "There's some talk about a hotel being built. Right now there's a big tent down a

15

ways that rents out cots."

"Have you got a, uh . . . ?" McConnell said.

"Oh yes," Clark said, grinning, "there's another tent at the other end of—of, I guess we can call this a street now, can't we? There's a whores' tent at the other end of the street."

"How many women?" McConnell asked.

"Three, and they're in demand. I guess you fellas know how badly a man wants a woman when he's been on the trail for a while."

"We've heard," McConnell said.

"Well, like I said, they're in demand, so they're expensive."

"Any other women in town?" McConnell asked.

"Some," Clark said. "Wives, daughters of people who have come here to start a business. Oh, and there are some Indian girls around."

A man came in and went to the counter rather than the bar, and Clark excused himself.

"Well, you've got your choice," McConnell said. "A whore or an Indian girl."

"That's supposing an Indian girl would say yes."

"Why wouldn't she?"

"Just the same, I think I'll skip it."

"Pike, this dream of yours—"

"It's not going to go away just because I sleep with a woman, Skins."

"That depends on the woman," McConnell said. "And besides, who said anything about sleeping?"

Chapter Two

Pike and McConnell pitched their own camp on the edge of "town," rather than rent a cot from the "hotel."

"What are you gonna do now?" McConnell asked.

"We need some supplies," Pike said. "I'll go and get them from Clark. What about you?"

"Well, I think I'll go and check out those whor— women. You know, just so I can tell you how they are, just in case you change your mind."

"I really appreciate that, Skins," Pike said wryly.

"Hey, what are friends for, right?" McConnell said and with a wave was off.

Pike got to Clark's just in time for the festivities.

Apparently, three trappers had just ridden in and were insistent that Ted Clark extend them some credit. Pike watched the argument from the door. Sky Woman was nowhere to be seen, probably in the back, which was just as well.

"Look, friend," one of the trappers said, "we're just a little short of funds. If you give us the credit we need, and the supplies, well then we can go out and earn the money to come back and pay you."

Clark listened, the doubt evident in his eyes.

"And I'm sure you'll come back and pay me, won't you?" Clark said. "I mean, that'll be the first thing on your mind, won't it?"

"Are you calling me a liar?" the first man asked.

He was the largest of the three, taller than Clark but not as tall as Pike. Of the other two, one was six feet tall but slender, and the other was under six feet, thickset, with legs like tree trunks. They stood on either side of the bigger man, who was either the only one who knew how to talk, or was simply their spokesman.

"I'm not calling you a liar, friend," Clark said. "I'm just telling you no credit."

"You only give credit to people you know, is that it?"

"No, I'm even more narrow-minded than that," Clark said. "I only give credit to my friends."

"Well, in that case," the man said, "let's be friends."

With that both he and his two friends produced their pistols and pointed them at Clark.

In the doorway Pike leveled his Hawken at them and notched back the hammer with an audible click.

"What . . . ?" the spokesman said, stiffening.

Smiling, Clark said to him, "I'd like you to meet one of my friends . . . *friend*."

The spokesman took a moment to consider the situation and then said, "He can't get all three of us."

18

"I'm holding a Hawken, friend," Pike said, "and the first one to die will be you—and there won't be much left to bury. The choice is yours."

As the man again considered the situation, Clark took the opportunity to bring his hand up from beneath his counter. In it he held a pistol, which had been trained on the middle man all the time.

"Now I suggest you boys get moving," he said, wiggling the pistol at them.

Pike could see only their backs, but he saw the spokesman's shoulders slump and knew the danger was past.

"Let's go," the spokesman said. The three men turned and saw Pike standing in the doorway. They put their pistols away and walked toward the door.

"I'm taking a good look at your face, mister," the spokesman said. He had a full red beard and one eye had gone milky white. Pike wondered if he could see out of it.

"I'll remember you, too, friend," Pike said, standing aside to let them pass.

The three men pushed past him and left. Pike stepped into the store and eased down the hammer on his Hawken.

"You ought to put up a sign, Ted," he said, approaching the counter.

"What kind? 'No vermin allowed'?" Clark asked, putting his pistol away.

" 'No credit.' "

They both laughed and Clark said, "Let me buy you a drink."

"No, I've had enough for a while," Pike said. "You can help me with this list, though."

Pike handed Clark a list of supplies he and McConnell needed and Clark took it.

"You want me to put this on your tab?"

"No," Pike said, laughing. "I'll pay cash."

"Your credit's good, Pike, you know that."

"Yeah, I know," Pike said, "but I'm afraid I'd feel just a wee bit guilty."

Clark began to fill his order and Pike looked around the store, waiting patiently. At that moment a woman walked through the door and he felt his eyes drawn to her. She was tall, full-bosomed, with long dark hair and full, lush lips. The thing that especially attracted him, though, was the whiteness of her skin. It made her dark eyes seem even darker. She appeared to be in her early thirties.

"Excuse me," she said to him, with a smile.

"Certainly," he said, stepping aside so she could approach the counter.

"Good afternoon, Mr. Clark," she said.

Clark turned around and Pike could see from the look in his friend's eyes that he was affected by this woman the same way he himself was.

"Hello, Mrs. Wilkes."

"I need some supplies," she said, handing him a list. It was considerably shorter than Pike's.

"Uh, well, ma'am, just let me finish with this gentleman and I'll—"

"No, that's all right, Ted," Pike said. "Take care of the lady first."

"Well, all right," Clark said with a smile. "It won't take long," he said to her.

She turned to Pike and said, "Thank you, Mister . . . ?"

"Pike, ma'am. My name is Pike, Jack Pike."

"Mr. Pike. It's refreshing to find a gentleman so far from the city."

"You're from the city, are you?"

"Yes, I am. I grew up in Denver, Colorado. Have you ever been there?"

"I'm afraid I haven't been much of anyplace, ma'am, but these mountains. I was born here."

"Really. How interesting. So many of the mountain men I run into came here from someplace else."

"Not me, ma'am. Born and raised in these mountains. My father, he came from somewhere else, although I can't for the life of me remember where. He died when I was very young."

"And your mother?"

"My mother was a Nez Percé squaw. After my pa died we lived with her people."

"An Indian woman!" Mrs. Wilkes said. "How interesting. How old were you when you started living with them?"

"Three, ma'am. Stayed until I was fourteen and my mother died, and then I went out on my own."

"And have you not been back—I mean, you haven't lived with the Nez Percé since then?"

"Oh, we've crossed tracks once or twice since then, ma'am. I can still count some of them as my friends."

"How marvelous," she said. "What a wonderfully colorful life you must have had up until now."

"Oh, a lot of it has been boring. Just a lot of hunting and trapping—"

"Boring to you, perhaps, but to someone who grew up in the city . . ."

"Here are your supplies, Mrs. Wilkes. I'll just put

21

it on your tab."

"Thank you, Mr. Clark," she said, accepting the bundle. She turned to Pike and said, "Mr. Pike, my name is Elizabeth Wilkes. I'd be honored if you'd come and see me before you left."

"Well, thank you, Mrs. Wilkes," Pike said. "Uh, I'll . . . I'll do that."

"Please do. Good day."

She left and Pike turned to look at Clark, who still had a glazed look in his eye.

"You'd better get that look out of your eyes before Sky Woman sees it."

"She's out walking," Clark said. "She won't be back for an hour or more."

"Who does she belong to?" Pike asked, jerking his head toward the door.

"Anybody who's got the price, I guess," Clark said.

"What?" Pike asked, shocked. "You mean that . . . that fine citified lady is a . . . a . . ."

"A whore," Clark said. "Come on, Pike. You can say the word. I've heard you use it before."

"Never to describe a woman like that."

"Well, like they say," Clark said, "it takes all kinds. Let me finish getting your supplies."

"Yeah," Pike said, still shaking his head in amazement, "sure . . ."

Chapter Three

The supplies turned out to be more than Pike could carry back to his tent himself, so Clark offered to help.

"What about business?"

"So I'll close for a few minutes," Clark said. "What are they gonna do, go somewhere else to get their supplies? Besides, maybe Sky Woman will get back before me and open up again."

Pike wagged a huge index finger at Clark and said, "You're getting too much power around here, Clark. It's going to your head."

"Power don't mean much to me, Pike," Clark said. "You know that."

"Mayor, sheriff . . . founder?" Pike said. "That's a lot of titles for one man."

"Founder?" Clark asked. "Of what?"

They moved the supplies out onto the front steps and Clark was locking his door.

"Don't you think this is going to build itself up into a town?" Pike asked. "A town called

Clark's Fork?''

"Pike, you know this area was called Clark's Fork before I got here," Clark said, picking up half the supplies. "It's one of the things that attracted me to settle here."

"Yeah, but who else knows that? Everybody thinks you're the Clark it's named after."

"I never claimed to be," Clark said. "Naw, this place looks okay now, Pike, but it ain't gonna get any bigger. You wait and see."

"Maybe you don't want it to get any bigger."

"What are you, a mind reader?" Clark asked.

They reached Pike's camp and put the supplies in the tent.

"Let me tell you something," Clark said, putting his hand on Pike's arm.

"Sit down," Pike said. He sat on his cot and Clark sat on McConnell's.

"When I set my business up here all I wanted to do was trade with Indians and some trappers. I came here to be alone, see? Then I met Sky Woman and she was all the company I wanted. This," he said, waving his arms, "this all came afterward, and I couldn't very well tell them not to settle here. I don't own the land."

"You could move on."

"Naw, I'm settled in here; Sky Woman's family is near here . . . we can't move on."

"So you're just hoping that interest around here will wane, huh?"

"If it doesn't . . . I guess I'll get rich, huh?"

Pike smiled and clapped his friend on the shoulder.

24

"I guess it could be worse, huh?"

"Sure," Clark said, standing up. "Well, let me get back to work. Where's McConnell?"

"Checking out those women you told me about . . . Hey, about this Mrs. Wilkes. Are you sure it's Mrs.?"

"She came here some months ago with her husband, and then he died. Heart attack, or something."

"And she turned to being a whore to make money?"

"To survive, Pike," Clark said, "to survive."

"You could have given her a job."

"Sure," Clark said, "tell that to Sky Woman. I'll see you later, Pike."

Skins McConnell watched the bobbing blond head of the whore as she worked on him, bringing him to full readiness again. He'd bet her an extra five dollars she couldn't do it, sure that he had exhausted himself beyond going at her a third time. She'd told him that her mouth could get anyone interested again, no matter how many times they'd been spent.

Now, as he felt himself rising again, he was amazed, and didn't even care that it was costing him another five dollars.

"Come on up here," he told her, reaching down and grabbing her beneath her arms.

She came up onto him, laughing, and impaled herself on him. He went into her wetness so easy and then she started riding him. He reached up and cupped her small but hard little breasts, flicking the nipples with his thumbs.

25

"I told you," she gasped, bouncing up and down on him, faster and faster, "I told you, I told you . . . Oh, I told you!"

Sky Woman was walking back to the trading post. She always took a walk in the late afternoon. She couldn't spend a whole day inside the trading post. The wooden walls started to close in on her.

Sky Woman was pretty, and she was young—too young, some had said, to marry Ted Clark—too pretty, some had said, to marry Ted Clark, the big bear of a white man—but she had married him, anyway. Her father and mother forgave her, her sister envied her. To Sky Woman none of that mattered. She loved Ted Clark, but every afternoon she had to go for a walk.

Now she was returning to the trading post.

The bear . . . the Indians . . . the guns that wouldn't fire . . .

Pike sat up and wiped the sweat from his face.

It was getting worse. Now he couldn't even try to catch up on the sleep the dream kept him from getting. Now the dream was coming to him even in a nap.

He got up and left the tent. The cold Rocky Mountain air felt even colder as it dried the sweat from his face.

He decided to go looking for Skins McConnell. Failing that he'd go and get a drink.

* * *

"Hey!"

"What?"

"Isn't that the squaw woman from the trading post?"

"Yeah, it looks like her."

"Well, well," the big trapper said. He looked at his two friends. "Maybe we'll get our credit from the squaw man after all—and maybe we'll get us something else, altogether."

The other two men watched the Indian woman admiringly, and nodded their heads.

Suddenly, a man appeared in Sky Woman's path.

"Hello, sweet thing," he said.

"Please," she said, "let me pass."

From behind her she heard a man say, "You don't like my friend? Maybe you'll like me."

She turned and saw that there was not one man behind her, but two. The man ahead of her was the largest of the three. It took a moment, but she recognized them from the trading post. She had just been leaving when they had entered.

"Please," she said, again, "let me pass."

"Let her pass," the first man said. "Boys, should we let her pass?"

"Hell, Jason," one of the other men said, "I can think of something better to do with her."

"Yeah," the man called Jason said, "so can I."

"Will you be back?" the blond whore asked McConnell.

"I don't know if I'll have time," he said, handing

her the money she'd earned—including the extra five. "Frankly, I don't know if I could live through it."

She laughed and blew him a kiss.

McConnell was walking back to the trading post when he saw the three men surrounding the Indian woman.

"Sky Woman," he said to himself, and then louder he called out, "Sky Woman!"

She looked over at him, but didn't move. She was afraid to move.

"Hey," he said, moving toward the three men and the Indian girl, "what's going on?"

The biggest of the three trappers turned to face him.

"What business is it of yours?"

"This lady happens to be a friend of mine."

"Is that a fact?" the man said. "Well, she was just gonna get real friendly with us, too. Come back in a little while and you can have her."

"No," McConnell said, "I think I'll take her with me now."

"Well, friend," the big man said, "I'm afraid you're gonna have yourself a time doing that. You see, there's three of us, and only one of you."

McConnell said, "I guess I'll just have to take my chances."

"Boys, no guns," the man called out to his friends. "This fella doesn't need to get dead, he just needs to be taught a lesson."

❀   ❀   ❀

28

Halfway between the trading post and the whores' tent Pike saw the fight.

"McConnell," he said, chastising his friend. That was when he saw Sky Woman, sitting on the ground, watching the fight, and then he recognized the three men McConnell was tangling with.

Suddenly, the fight was a little more serious than a possible difference of opinion.

Pike rushed forward to help his friend. Two of the men were holding McConnell now, and as the bigger man drew back a fist to hit him, Pike hooked his arm and pulled, causing the man to tumble to the ground. He stepped in then and hit one of the men holding McConnell. McConnell then swung the other man around and hit him.

Pike turned in time to catch the rush of the bigger man. He had his head down and buried it in Pike's midsection. Both men fell to the ground, and then scrambled to be the first one up. Pike made it first and hit the other man as he was trying to get to his feet. The man went down and Pike finished him with a well-placed kick.

He turned and saw McConnell grappling with the other two men. He went over and pulled one away from his friend. In five seconds the two men were lying on the ground, one on top of the other.

"What was this all about?" Pike asked McConnell.

McConnell wiped blood from his mouth with the back of his hand and looked at it.

"They were fixing to rape Sky Woman, from the looks of it."

"I guess that'd be their way of getting back at Clark for not extending them credit."

McConnell made a face.

"They'd rape a man's wife for that?"

"I guess they would."

Pike bent over each man and relieved them of their pistols.

"I'll take these three to their horses and get them on their way. You take Sky Woman back to the trading post."

"Why are you gonna turn them loose?"

"Because if I don't," Pike said, "Clark is liable to kill the three of them."

"Well, he's the law here."

"The unofficial law," Pike reminded him. "No, I think we're better off sending them on their way than letting Clark kill three men."

"I guess you're right. I'll see you back there."

McConnell helped Sky Woman to her feet. Pike went over to the men and kicked all three of them awake.

"Let's go, fellas," he said. "You have a long walk ahead of you."

Pike put one of their pistols in his belt and kept the other two in hand, covering them as they staggered to their feet.

The big one wiped his bloody mouth on his sleeve and said, "Whataya think you're doin'?"

"I'm escorting you and your friends to the city limits, friend," Pike said.

"What city?"

"It's just a figure of speech, son," Pike said. "Let's get walking."

"Our horses are in the livery."

"I changed my mind about that," Pike said. "You're walking."

30

"What?" one of the others said, his jaw falling.

"You can't put us out there afoot," the big man said.

"What's your name?"

"Jason Burns," the big man said.

"Well, Jason, you look like a gent who has spent some time in the mountains."

"Most of my life."

"Then you'll know how to survive until you reach a settlement, or a Crow or Blackfoot camp. Hell, you might even find a wild horse or two."

"Listen, mister—" one of the other men started.

"Enough talk," Pike said. "Either you start walking or you die right here."

"You wouldn't," Burns said.

"Try me," Pike said, and pointed the man's own gun at him. "From here I can't miss. I'll give you a third eye, friend. Walk or die."

"We'll walk, we'll walk," one of the other men said. "Come on, Jace."

Pike walked them to the edge of the trading post and then stopped.

"This is as far as I go, friends."

"You can't put us afoot without a gun."

"You're right about that," Pike said. He pointed one of the guns at Burns and pulled the trigger. The man cried out and cringed as the ball flew past his ear. Pike tossed the empty gun to the man, who just barely managed to catch it, and then took the third gun out of his belt and filled his empty hand.

"Now you got a gun. You boys can load up as soon as you're far away from here."

"Mister," one of the men said, "you're killin' us."

"No," Pike said, "that's what I should be doing, and that's what Sky Woman's man will do if you don't leave. Any man who'd rape a woman—and another man's woman, at that—deserves to die. I'm being charitable, only you boys just don't see it. Now move!"

"C'mon, Jace," one of the other men said, and the second man grabbed Jason Burns's arm.

"Friend, you better kill me now, 'cause I'll kill you next time I see you," Burns said to Pike, shaking with rage.

"My name is Pike, son," Pike said. "Anytime you want to come look me up, you do that, hear?"

"Jace!"

The other two men pulled on Jason Burns until they got him moving, and Pike watched them walk until they were out of sight.

As he tucked both of the remaining pistols into his belt he knew that the man called Jason Burns was right.

He should have killed them—or at least, he should have killed Burns. He'd made himself another enemy—a dangerous one—which was something Jack Pike didn't need.

Chapter Four

When Pike returned to Clark's store Sky Woman and McConnell had apparently told their stories, and Pike thought Clark was remarkably calm until he realized that the word "rape" had not been used. It seemed that McConnell and Sky Woman had decided to play down that part of the incident. Instead, they simply told Clark that the three men were harassing her, and talking about trading her for some supplies.

"Where are they?" Clark demanded as Pike entered. He had his right arm around his wife's shoulders. "Wife" was a word used loosely in the mountains, since there was no preacher for miles. Still and all, Clark considered Sky Woman his wife, and no one was going to tell him different.

"They're gone."

"You let them go free?"

"I did," Pike said, setting the two pistols on the counter. "But they've only got one pistol among 'em, and they're afoot."

A wide grin spread over Ted Clark's face and he

tightened his arm around Sky Woman.

"You see this man, Sky Woman? This man is downright evil, I tell you," Clark said, with glee. "Me, I would have killed those men, but not ol' Pike. He lets them go . . . afoot! If that don't beat all."

"They'll survive," Pike said.

"Maybe," Clark said, "and maybe not, but you know I would have killed them."

"I know that."

"And you saved me from that grief," Clark said. "I thank you for that, Pike," he added, extending his hand, "and I thank both of you," he went on, giving his hand to McConnell, "for what you done."

"It was McConnell here who decided to take on the three of them by himself. Typical of the dumb kind of move he generally makes."

"Oh yeah?" McConnell asked. "And who was it rode into a Blackfoot camp a few months back and took on six braves by himself, all to protect a woman's honor?"

Clark looked at Pike and said, "You did that?"

"They were Crow and there were five of them," Pike said. He inclined his head toward Sky Woman and said, "Excuse me, Sky Woman."

She shook her head at him and said, "You have no cause to apologize to me. You must have had good reason for what you did."

"Sure he did," Clark said, "the same reason he and McConnell helped you today. Neither of them can stand to see a damsel in distress. You really rode in on five Crow—in their own camp?"

"I was mad," Pike said. "Sylvia Bodeen is a good friend and they were . . . bothering her."

He didn't bother telling them that the Crow were not only bothering Sylvia, but "using." That was between him and Sylvia, and nobody else's business.

"You see, honey, these two boys are—"

"Can we get off this subject?" McConnell asked. "You got a cold beer I can hold up to my mouth before it swells up?"

"Comin' up—and on the house!"

"I will get them," Sky Woman said, and hurried to the bar.

"She's a fine woman," Clark said. "I got—"

"Don't thank us again, Ted," Pike said, warning.

Clark held both hands up in surrender and said, "Sorry, sorry. No more messy gratitude."

Sky Woman came back with the beers, then excused herself to go to the kitchen.

"Where can I find a card game around here?" McConnell asked.

"There's a legit saloon tent across the street. I don't do much drinkin' business since they opened up, but I don't mind. All the likkered-up troublemakers end up over there—and so do the card players."

"That's where I'm heading," McConnell said. "You comin', Pike?"

"Maybe later," Pike said. "I'll just finish this up and go for a walk."

"Here, finish mine, too," McConnell said. "I'll see you later."

"Good luck."

After McConnell left Pike sipped his beer, deep in thought.

"You fellas waitin' on anybody?"

Pike nodded.

"Whiskey Sam and Dick Post."

"I know Sam, but don't know Post."

"I'll introduce you," Pike said, putting his empty mug down.

"You gona finish his?" Clark asked.

"No, I think I'll just walk."

"Where to?"

"Nowhere in particular."

Pike turned and walked to the door and as he was going out he heard Clark say, "Nowhere in particular, my ass!"

Chapter Five

Pike walked down to where the whores' tent was. He loitered outside for a while, watching the comings and goings of men, catching glimpses of the women inside. Finally, as it started to get dark, he tossed aside the tent flap and walked inside.

From the outside the tent was huge, but inside it was sectioned off into smaller "cribs." He'd seen such cribs before at rendezvous, but they had been made of wood. Standing there just inside the entrance he could hear the sounds of the whores doing their business. He was about to turn and walk out when a woman came out of one of the cribs and saw him.

"Hey, big man!" she called.

He turned and watched her walk toward him. She was big-breasted and wide-hipped, and looked to be in her forties. Her face was hard, but had once been handsome. He wondered if she were simply the madam, or if she was still a working gal.

"Where are you going?" she asked.

"I, uh, was going out—"

"Without getting what you come for?" she asked. She put her hands on his shoulder and said, "Big man like you, I should let my girls come out and fight over you instead of giving you your choice of them."

"I, uh, changed my mind—"

"Without seeing my girls? Believe me, handsome, I got some beauties." She leaned closer to him and said, "I got a blond virgin, barely seventeen."

He doubted that very much.

"I wasn't—I mean, I was looking for a certain woman."

"Oh, heard about my girls, eh?" she said, proudly. "Which one did you hear about?"

"Her name is Elizabeth Wilkes."

"That one!" the woman said, frowning. "Believe me, honey, you don't want her. She's uppity, that one. Only works when she wants to. I only keep her around because she's classy-looking, but looks ain't everything, you know. Take me, fer instance. I could give you a ride you'd write home about—"

"I'd like to see Elizabeth, please," he said.

She frowned up at him, hands on her ample hips, and then shrugged.

"Ah, hell, I'll tell her you're here."

As she started away he called out, "Don't you want to know my name?"

"It ain't necessary, honey," she called back, with a negligent wave of her pudgy hand.

"Pike!" he said. "Tell her it's Pike!"

She waved again and continued on down a makeshift hall. After a moment she disappeared into one of the "cribs," and then reappeared a moment later.

"You're in luck, handsome," she said, waving at him. "She'll see you."

Oh Lord, he said, not here. But he went ahead and walked toward the madam.

"Right in here, handsome," she said, holding back the flap on the crib, leering at him. "Enjoy yourself."

He ducked his head and entered, then stood straight up. The inside was barely eight feet by eight feet and badly lit by a storm lamp. Elizabeth Wilkes was standing there next to a sagging cot, fully dressed, a smile of welcome on her lips.

"Hello, Pike."

"Mrs. Wilkes—"

"Please, call me Elizabeth," she said. "I'm glad you came to see me."

"To be very honest, Elizabeth," he said, "I'm not so sure I am."

She stared at him for a few moments, then wrinkled her nose and said, "I know what you mean. It's disgusting, isn't it?"

At that moment a man wailed somewhere, followed by a woman's cry. The woman's cry probably was supposed to sound like one of pleasure, but she merely sounded tired and bored.

"That's Lucy," Elizabeth Wilkes said. "She's no actress at all, but the men don't seem to mind."

"Look, Elizabeth," he said, backing away, "I shouldn't have come here—"

"Wait," she said, moving forward and putting her hand on his arm to stay him. "Can I come with you?"

"Well—"

"We can walk, and talk . . . and see what happens. I want to get out of here, anyway."

39

She smiled at him, and instantly won him over.

"All right," he said, "but what about . . . what's her name?"

"That's Katy. She won't care. If she says anything, I'll quit. Let me get my shawl." She went to the cot, picked it up and tossed it around her shoulders. "All right, let's go."

He gave her his arm and she took it, and they walked out together.

They walked for a short while, talking about nothing in particular. Pike felt himself tongue-tied by this lovely woman who certainly belonged in a lot of places, none of them here.

Suddenly, he noticed that she was shivering and damned himself.

"You're cold," he said. "I'm sorry. We can go back—"

"No, I don't want to go back," she insisted. "Perhaps if you put your arm around me?"

"Sure," he said, feeling big and clumsy as he slid his right arm around her shoulders.

"Pike?"

"Yes?"

"Do you have a tent of your own?"

"Y-yes, at the far end of the settlement. I mean, my partner and I—"

"What's your partner doing?"

"Playing poker."

"Will he be doing that for some time?"

"Knowing him, I'm sure he will—"

"Can we go to your tent?"

"My tent?"

"You know," she said, sliding her arm around his waist, "to finish our . . . talk?"

"Well—" he stammered.

"And to warm up."

"I, uh—"

"Together," she said, tightening her arm around him.

Oh hell, he thought.

"Let's go to my tent."

"What a marvelous idea!"

Chapter Six

When they entered his tent he lit the lamp and turned to face her. She moved close to him—so close their bodies touched—and took his face in her hands.

"I want you to know there's no charge for this," she said, rubbing his face. "I'm here because I want to be."

"That's funny," he said, putting his arms around her waist, "I'm here for the same reason."

As they kissed he suddenly felt less clumsy. There were buttons at the back of her dress and he started undoing them. Her hands went to his shirt, pulled it from his pants and burrowed under it, only to encounter his long underwear. She scratched him through it, and moaned into his mouth, pushing her tongue past his lips.

He started to peel the dress down over her shoulders when he felt her shiver and he felt goosebumps rise on her flesh.

"Wait," he said.

"I can't," she said against his mouth.

"I'll light a fire."

"In here?"

He smiled and said, "It'll warm the place. You'll see."

He and McConnell had already rounded up as many round stones as they could find, fist-size. Pike set them in a circle on the ground in the middle of the floor, then tossed some wood chips they'd found into the center and lit the fire.

"That's wonderful," she said. "The fire will heat the stones."

"That's right," he said, standing up. "It'll be warmer in here in a few minutes."

"I can't wait," she said. "Let it get warm while we . . . warm ourselves."

She slid the dress off her shoulders and dropped it to the ground. No wonder she had been shivering. She was completely naked underneath—and now she was completely naked . . . period. She was a big woman, with large, almost pear-shaped breasts and wide hips. For a big man like Pike it was almost a prerequisite with him that a woman be big—like Elizabeth Wilkes.

The sight of her made Pike catch his breath. She walked up to him and started to unbutton his shirt.

"I can do this faster than you can," he said, catching her hands at the wrists. His hands itched to palm her big breasts, yet he was savoring the anticipation.

"I'd like to do it."

"If I do it," he said, "we'll get under the blanket faster."

"On that cot?" she asked. "It's not much better

44

than the one back at . . . the one I have."

"Watch," he said.

He took the blanket off his cot and spread it on the floor, near the fire. Then he took an extra blanket from his gear and spread that one, then folded it down halfway.

"Our bed," he said.

"Well, get undressed so we can use it," she said. "I'm getting awfully impatient."

"Yes," he said, "suddenly so am I."

He undressed quickly and she watched with pleasure. He was not only a big man, but a well-muscled man, and she enjoyed watching the way his muscles moved. When he was naked she moved forward and wrapped her hands around his impressive erection.

"Do I have to yell timber?" she asked.

She yelled, but "timber" wasn't what she yelled.

"Jesus," she said, her legs wrapped around his waist. "Oh Christ, it feels like you're in me all the way up to my chest!"

"We can go easy," he said. He had a hand on either side of her, holding his full weight off her as he moved inside her.

"No, no," she said, grabbing hold of his buttocks as if he'd threatened to withdraw, "not easy. Just go, just . . . go . . . and . . . go!"

"You don't have to do this, you know," he told her as she leaned down between his legs.

45

"Oh, Pike," she said. "I want to, can't you see that?"

He was about to answer when she took him in her mouth and froze the words in his mouth. Her head bobbed up and down as she took more and more of him into her mouth, cupping his sack in one hand while holding the base of his penis with the other.

"Mmmm," she moaned around him, and he guessed that she really did want to do it for him—and maybe for herself, too.

He took her head in his hands gently and decided to stop questioning the situation and just enjoy it.

Still later she was atop him, lying on him, moving her hips frantically as he palmed her big, smooth buttocks.

"Oh yes," she groaned. "Oh Jesus, yes, here it comes . . . come with me, baby, come with me . . ."

As he emptied himself into her she moaned aloud and he knew she wanted to scream but was holding it in. He squeezed her ass as she milked him, grunting and groaning to get every last drop from him that she could.

They were all there . . .
. . . the Indians . . .
. . . the guns that wouldn't shoot . . .
. . . the snow beneath his feet . . .
. . . but as he looked back a last time something else was there, something that was new to the dream.

46

It was a woman . . .

. . . she was naked, lying on the snow between him and the grizzly, smiling at him—smiling, damn it!—as the grizzly bore down on her . . .

. . . he turned and ran back toward her, toward the damned grizzly, waiting for the Indians to fire, waiting for lead balls to slam into his flesh . . .

. . . this was different . . .

. . . it was the same dream, but different . . .

Why was Elizabeth Wilkes in this dream?

"Hey, are you all right?"

He was sitting up, his body drenched in sweat.

"Jesus, you're going to catch your death of cold," she said. She grabbed the blanket and wrapped it around him, holding him tight.

"It's all right," she whispered into his ear, "it was only a dream, it's all right."

"It wasn't only a dream," he said. "It was the same damned dream!"

Chapter Seven

"Where did you sleep last night?" Pike asked McConnell at breakfast. He was feeling guilty because Elizabeth Wilkes had stayed with him all night. He also wondered what McConnell had heard or seen when he finally returned to the tent.

"Don't worry about me," McConnell said. "I found a place."

They were at Ted Clark's, eating a wonderful breakfast that had been prepared by Sky Woman, for which Clark would accept no money.

"When I came back to the tent with my considerable winnings," McConnell went on, "I heard this commotion going on inside. I took a look—"

"You looked?"

"Hey," McConnell said, spreading his hands, "you might have been in trouble."

"I wasn't."

"Well, I found that out," McConnell said. He was trying to keep a straight face. "I saw this big, beautiful butt humping up and down—"

"Don't talk about her like that," Pike said. "She's a very nice woman."

McConnell grinned and said, "Who said I was talking about *her* butt?"

"You're a disgusting old man, do you know that?"

"Hey, I got mine," McConnell said. "It was only right that you got yours."

"Thanks."

"Of course, you got more than I did, and probably paid less for it—"

"A lot less."

"Like nothing?"

"Like nothing."

McConnell shook his head.

"Why do women like you, Pike?"

"They like the little boy in me."

"Maybe, but that sure ain't the side they get, is it?"

"Shhh!" Pike said, as Sky Woman approached with more eggs.

"Please," she said, grinning happily at them, "eat more. Can I bring you some more coffee?"

"Thank you, Sky Woman," Pike said.

After she left McConnell said, "Did you sleep?"

"Yes."

"And?"

"And I had the dream."

"The same damned dream?"

"The same dream . . . but different."

"What do you mean, different?"

Pike put his fork down to concentrate on the telling of the dream.

"There was a woman in it."

"What woman?"

50

"That woman," Pike said. "The woman I was with, Elizabeth Wilkes."

"What was she doing there?"

Pike shrugged helplessly and described the dream for his friend in detail. He paused when Sky Woman returned with another pot of coffee.

"Well," McConnell said after Sky Woman left them again, "this could be encouraging, you know."

"What do you mean?"

"Well, I mean the dream has changed, hasn't it? It wasn't exactly the same."

"No . . ."

"What do you mean 'no'?" McConnell asked. "It was the same or it wasn't."

"I mean it was exactly the same up to a point . . . and then it continued on, and that's where Elizabeth Wilkes came in."

"You mean the dream went on longer this time?"

"Right."

"But . . . but what if it had gone on longer one of the other times? She wouldn't have been in it then . . . would she?" McConnell asked, doubtfully. "I mean, if she was it would be . . . even crazier."

"I know," Pike said. "That's the word I keep thinking of."

"What word?"

"Crazy."

"Aw, Pike, you ain't crazy."

"Then what am I?"

"I don't know . . ." McConnell said.

"Yeah," Pike said. He sipped some coffee and said, "When are Sam and Dick supposed to be in?"

"They'll be here by noon, unless they ran into

51

some trouble."

"Let's be ready to leave by then, whether they show or not. They can catch up to us. They know we're going up onto the fork." He stood up and said, "I'm going for a walk."

"Go ahead. I'm going to finish this coffee."

As Pike left Ted Clark came over to the table and sat with him.

"How was breakfast?"

"It was fine, Ted, real fine."

"Skins . . . what's eating at Pike?"

McConnell put his cup down and looked at Clark.

"You noticed, huh?"

"Can't help but. He spends a lot of time looking off into space at something the rest of us can't see."

"It's up to him to tell you, Ted," McConnell said. "Let's just say he's been having a dream . . . the same dream . . . night after night . . ."

Clark frowned.

"It don't much matter what the dream is," he said. "That'd rattle any man. Will he talk about it?"

"He's talked to me, and it hasn't done much good," McConnell said. Then he brightened, as something occurred to him.

"Ted, don't the Indians interpret dreams?"

"Some dreams," Clark said, "and some Indians. Are you thinking about Sky Woman?"

"Yes."

"Would he talk to her?"

"Maybe . . . maybe if we asked him . . ."

"Maybe if she asked him," Clark said. "To tell you the truth, she's the one noticed something was bothering him."

"Would she do it?"

"I think she would," Clark said. "I'll put it to her."

"We'll be pulling out at noon, Ted, whether or not Sam and Dick get here."

"I'll talk to her now," Clark said, standing up.

"I appreciate it."

Clark nodded and went to talk to Sky Woman.

McConnell hoped that maybe they had found the answer for Pike.

Chapter Eight

Out walking, alone with his thoughts, Pike was very surprised when he turned and found Sky Woman almost upon him. He smiled, waiting for her to reach him.

"Sky Woman," he said.

"Pike," she replied. She stopped right in front of him and he realized how very small she was. It made the union between her and Clark even more . . . unlikely, and yet they obviously loved each other very much.

"You are troubled," she said to him, touching his arm. "I have felt it ever since you arrived."

He stared into her eyes, prepared to put her off, and then said, "Yes, I am troubled."

"By a dream?"

He looked surprised, then became suspicious.

"Has McConnell been talking to you?"

"McConnell is a good friend to you," she said, "but he did not have to say anything. I asked Clark to find out, and he talked to McConnell."

"And he told about the dream?"

"Only that there was one," she said. She moved away from him, then turned and looked at him over her shoulder. "He did not tell *of* the dream. He said that would be up to you—if you wished."

"And are you then to try and interpret the dream?"

"Have you attempted to have someone do so?"

"No."

"And do you wish me to do so?"

"I would not have presumed to ask—"

"That is nonsense," she said. She returned to him and put her hand on his arm again. "You are our very great friend. It would honor me if you would allow me to try and help you."

He took her hand and said, "Thank you, Sky Woman."

"Come," she said, squeezing his hand, "we will find someplace to sit where we will not be disturbed."

She seemed to know just the place and led him there by the hand. It was out of sight of the settlement, and there were a couple of large stones they could sit on.

"Please," she said, once they were seated, "tell me about the dream."

Pike talked, then, telling her what the dream was about. Afterward she asked him to describe to her each incarnation of the dream, up to last night's, when someone else managed to intrude herself on the dream.

"You say that as if Elizabeth invaded my dream willingly," Pike said.

"Not at all. I only mean that someone else appeared in your dream."

"Well, that's true enough. Do you know what it means?"

"It does not have to mean anything," she said, "but I did notice—have you told me of each dream exactly as it occurred?"

"Yes. I remember them vividly."

"That is good."

There was an awkward moment of silence and Pike was not sure whether he was to speak or not. Finally, Sky Woman broke the silence.

"I have noticed," she said, speaking very precisely, "that each time you have had the dream it has gone on a little longer."

Pike started, surprised, then frowned and thought about it.

"Yes," he said, "now that you mention it, it does seem that way."

"And last night it went on long enough for someone else to appear."

"But why her?"

Sky Woman shrugged.

"Because she was with you. Perhaps, if she had not been there, you would have dreamed of someone else in danger—someone close to you, someone you had known in the past. It probably would not even have had to be a woman. A friend, perhaps—like McConnell."

"It still bothers me that it was Elizabeth, whom I only just met."

Sky Woman smiled at him.

"She must have made a very great impression on you, Pike."

"Well . . . she did, actually. I like her. I don't think

57

she belongs here."

"I know the woman of whom we are speaking, and I agree. She does not belong here, at all."

"Still, none of this explains the dream."

"I did not say I could explain it," she said, "although in time, I might be able to."

"I can't stay," he said. "I can't allow the dream to change my life."

"And so you should not," she said. "Perhaps I should only tell you that with my people, dreams are nothing to be feared. I am Crow, but you've lived with the Nez Percé, so you no doubt know that."

"I do . . . it's just difficult not to be afraid."

"And it is natural," she said, "but I think I can safely say that you were not going mad—if that helps."

He reached for her hand and said, "It does. I thank you for taking the time to listen, and to talk to me."

"It is I who thank you for trusting me," she said. "It is a very great honor."

They rose together and she said, "Perhaps we should go back now. You are waiting for friends to arrive."

"Yes."

"And perhaps you should talk to someone else."

"Who?"

Sky Woman smiled enigmatically and started to lead him back to the settlement.

Maybe she meant Elizabeth Wilkes. He'd been thinking about talking to her, only he wasn't sure what about.

Maybe the subject would take care of itself.

Chapter Nine

When Pike and Sky Woman got back to the trading post, Ted Clark and Skins McConnell had company —Whiskey Sam and Dick Post.

"Pike, you ol' polecat!" Whiskey Sam said.

Pike smiled and shook hands with Sam, who could have been fifty, sixty or more. He'd never tell.

Pike went on to Dick Post and shook hands. Post was in his thirties and usually did his hunting alone. Pike was surprised that he had agreed to come along this time.

"How are you, Dick?"

"Doing well, Pike. You ready to go?"

"Just about," Pike said. He looked at McConnell and said, "Why don't you have Sam and Dick help you get our gear together?"

"And you?"

"I have to talk to someone."

"Oh," McConnell said. "Okay, boys, right this way. Mr. Pike wants us to do his packing for him."

"Gettin' high and mighty, is he?" Whiskey Sam

asked. "Let me finish my drink and we'll get right to it."

"I'll meet you in a few minutes," Pike said, and left.

Clark and McConnell looked at Sky Woman, who didn't say anything. Whiskey Sam and Dick Post finished their drinks without sensing anything in the air. Sky Woman went into the back without saying a word. McConnell and Clark exchanged shrugs. McConnell figured he'd find out what happened from Pike, while Sky Woman would probably talk to Clark after they had all gone.

He figured Pike was going to talk to Elizabeth Wilkes, but he had no idea what the outcome of that talk would be.

Neither had Pike, when he left.

Pike walked to the big tent and went inside. At that moment a naked blonde was walking through the tent and stopped when she saw him. She was carrying a towel, and was either coming from or going to a bath. The cold didn't seem to bother her, and her nakedness didn't bother her, either.

"Hel-lo," she said. She turned and came up to stand real close to him. She was pretty, and well built along slimmer lines than Elizabeth. She was also younger, but that was not necessarily automatically in her favor.

"Is Elizabeth around?" he asked.

"Mmm," the girl said, "she gets the big ones, huh?" She moved up against him, crushing her breasts against him. She was playing the role of

60

whore to the hilt, and he had the feeling that she truly liked it. In fact, from the scent she was exuding, it excited her—and he felt himself reacting, also. "I know what to do with the big ones."

"Maybe another time," he said. "Right now I'd like to see Elizabeth."

"Only have eyes for her ladyship, huh?" she asked, bumping her crotch up against him. He could feel her heat right through his clothes. "Honey, you have no idea what you're missing."

Pike flexed his fingers, wanting to grab ahold of this girl. Maybe what he did need was a good, mindless roll with a girl who found it the only way to truly express herself. He did want to see Elizabeth, though, and he did have people waiting for him.

"Uh, aren't you closed now?" he asked.

"Baby," she said, licking her lips elaborately, "I'm never closed."

"Colette!"

Pike turned his head and saw the madam standing with her hands on her hips. She was wearing some kind of a fuzzy, furry robe.

"Colette?" he asked.

"It's not my real name," the blonde said. "Come back later and I'll tell you my real name."

"Go and take your bath, Colette," the woman called out. "And better make it a cold one."

Colette gave Pike a teasing look, touched her finger to her tongue, wetting it, and then pressed it to his lips.

"Just a taste," she said, and walked away. He watched her bare buttocks twitch until she was out of sight.

"You have admirable restraint," the madam said to Pike. "When she gets that aggressive I've never seen a man who could resist her."

"I'd like to see Elizabeth."

"Mmm," the madam said, "that explains it, then. Go on back. I don't think she'll mind."

Pike walked to the back to Elizabeth's crib.

"Elizabeth?"

"Pike?" her voice came from inside. She sounded pleased. "Come on in."

He pushed aside the blanket door and entered. She was seated on the cot, wearing a much simpler robe than the madam—although it did show quite a bit of her legs and thighs.

"Pike, how nice," she said. "Come and sit."

Pike sat next to her.

"I ran into a friend of yours," he said.

"Who?"

"Colette."

Elizabeth made a face.

"She's no friend of mine. Was she naked?"

"As the day she was born."

"Did she attack you?"

"Just about."

"That bitch is always in heat," she said. "She loves this job."

"And you?"

"I hate it. I hardly ever meet a man like you in here, gentle, tender."

"You don't belong here, Elizabeth."

"I know that."

"Why don't you leave?"

"With what? I've only got a little money, and I'd

have to buy a horse."

"I'll give you a horse," Pike said. "And some money."

She smiled.

"Why, Pike?"

"Because I like you. Because I want to see you out of here."

"You're so sweet," she said. She leaned over and kissed him on the cheek. For all of Colette's rubbing, Elizabeth's simple kiss affected him more. "I can't do that, Pike."

"I want to help you."

"I know," she said, taking his hand. She lowered her head, then squeezed his hand and looked at him. "There is a way you can help me."

"How?"

"Take me with you."

"With me?" he said, laughing. "I'm going on a buffalo hunt."

"Take me with you," she said. "Teach me. If I can learn something, a different way to make a living, then I can get out of here."

"Elizabeth, a buffalo hunt is not an easy thing," he said. "There are hardships, dangers—"

"Anything has to be better than this, Pike," she said, putting her head on his shoulder. "I guess I'm being unfair, asking this of you."

Just then he thought of the dream. He'd started thinking that maybe the dream was something that was going to come true. How could Elizabeth be in his dream if he didn't take her along?

"No," he said, "you're not asking too much."

"You mean . . . you'll take me?"

63

"Anything to get you out of here."

"What about your friends?" she asked. "What will they say?"

"I don't know," he said. "I guess we'll find out. Have you got some warm clothes?"

"Yes."

He fingered her robe and said, "Leave all this stuff behind. Just take whatever you have that's thick and warm."

"All right," she said, excitedly. "It won't take me long."

"Have you ever fired a rifle?"

"Yes."

"All right. I'll get you a rifle, and a horse, and I'll meet you back here in half an hour."

"I'll be ready," she promised.

Pike left the tent, wondering how he was going to explain this to the others.

Chapter Ten

"You want to what?" McConnell asked.

"Take her with us."

"What for?"

"Well, for a few reasons, but most of all . . . I want to get her out of there."

"And?"

"Maybe she'll catch on."

"And what? Hunt buffalo for a living?"

"It's better than selling herself."

"If she wasn't selling herself you never would have gotten to know her."

"So, just because one good thing comes out of it doesn't make it right."

McConnell frowned. Whiskey Sam and Dick Post were loading their gear onto their mules for them and couldn't hear the conversation.

"What about Sam and Dick?" McConnell said.

"Well, if they object they hunt on their own. Listen, Skins, if you object you can ride along with them. I don't want to—"

"No, hey, no," McConnell said. "I don't object. Besides, I'd like to be around when you find out what that dream really means."

Pike clapped his friend on the shoulder and said, "Let's see how Whiskey Sam and Dick feel about it."

To their surprise Whiskey Sam and Dick Post had no objection.

"Can she cook?" Sam asked.

"Sure she can cook," Pike said, although he had no idea whether she could or not.

"Then bring her along," he said. He looked at Post, who nodded.

"Thanks, boys."

"No problem," Sam said. "Just, let's get going."

"I'll pick her up right now."

Pike went to Ted Clark's next, and found Clark waiting for him with a completely outfitted horse, and a rifle, a Hawken like Pike's, but older and not as well cared-for.

"I figured you could teach her better with a familiar weapon."

"I appreciate this, Ted."

"Forget it," Clark said. "After what you did for Sky Woman, this is nothing."

"Let me pay you—"

"Not a cent, Pike. Get out of here."

Pike shook hands with Clark and Sky Woman came out the door behind Clark.

"Sky Woman—"

"I am sorry I could not tell you what the dream meant, Pike," she said, "but I think you will find out soon."

Pike frowned at her, wondering if she really did know and just didn't want to tell him, for some reason. Well, if that was the case, he'd respect her wishes.

"Thank you, Sky Woman."

"Come back this way, Pike, and tell us what the answer was."

"I will," he said.

"Good luck on the hunt," Clark said.

Pike took the reins and the rifle and walked away.

When he reached the tent he found Elizabeth waiting outside. She was wearing pants and a heavy jacket, and had an old hat on.

"Hi," she said. "The hat and jacket were my husband's. He wasn't a big man, like you. I'm sure he wouldn't mind."

"This horse is yours," he said.

"He's beautiful."

The animal was actually less than beautiful. It was nine years old and had seen better days, but it was an Indian pony, and knew its way around the mountains.

"And this is your rifle," he said, handing it to her. He also gave her a hunting pouch and powder horn.

"You know what these are?"

"I know what the powder horn is for, but not the other."

"All right," he said. "When we get started we'll ride side by side. I'll talk and you'll listen . . . and learn. Is that understood?"

"It's understood."

"Then mount up," he said, then looked at her and

said, "You can ride, can't you?"

"Oh sure," she said. "I used to ride some back in Denver."

She mounted and he handed her the reins. She handled them with ease, and any fears he had about her not riding well disappeared. At least she wouldn't hold them up.

"I really appreciate this, Pike."

"It's all right," he said. "Oh, by the way, you'll have to earn your keep."

"How?"

"Can you cook?"

"Some."

"That's got to be better than the rest of us."

She didn't reply, and as they started back to meet the rest of the party he hoped that she'd at least be able to cook a little better than the rest of them.

When they reached the others they were all mounted and waiting. Pike counted seven pack mules, which meant that Whiskey Sam and Dick Post had each brought one.

"This the lady?" Sam said. From the gleam in his eyes the old hunter obviously approved.

Pike allowed as how she was the lady and made the introductions.

"Pike says you can cook," Whiskey Sam said.

Elizabeth threw Pike a look, then said to Sam, "Uh, yes, I can cook."

"What do we call you?"

She smiled at him—winning him over instantly, Pike noticed—and said, "You can call me Liz."

"Well, Liz, there's buffalo out there waiting for us," Whiskey Sam said.

"In that case," she said, "I suggest we get moving before someone else gets there first."

"She can cook," Sam said, "she's good-looking, and she's smart. Maybe we should leave you behind, Pike."

"This hunt was my idea," Pike pointed out.

Sam looked at Elizabeth—who would be "Liz" from now on—and said, "I knew he'd find an excuse to come along."

PART TWO

THE HUNT

Chapter Eleven

The weather was cold and clear, and the snow beneath their horses' hooves was only three or four inches deep. Pike let Whiskey Sam take the point and lagged back to ride side-by-side with Liz whenever he could, to conduct their lessons. As they had agreed, he talked and she listened—and he had to admit that she listened very well.

The first night out she cooked. Pike had advised her to keep it simple, so she made some beans and bacon and broke out some biscuits they'd gotten from Clark, and dinner went over very big with Whiskey Sam and Dick Post.

"Yes, sir," Sam said, "nothing like a woman's touch to make a dinner taste better. Right, Dick?"

"You got that right, Sam," Post said, sopping up some bacon grease with a biscuit.

Later, they also raved over her coffee, which, Pike was pleasantly surprised to find, was delicious.

Liz looked at Pike and smiled conspiratorially. Later, when he was helping her clean the plates with some snow, she said, "I can't make bacon and beans every night."

"If you make coffee like that every night, you won't have to worry about that. Don't worry about the cooking, Liz. These boys will enjoy anything that's hot. We'll probably also come across some game along the way. There aren't too many ways to ruin rabbit."

"When we find some buffalo will I be able to take a shot?"

"We'll find that out tomorrow."

"What happens tomorrow?"

"Tomorrow we'll find out if you can shoot."

After they had put away the cooking untensils they built another fire, a larger one, for warmth. The smaller fire accommodated the coffeepot.

"Liz and I will sleep around the smaller fire," Pike said. "You boys can have the larger one."

"We should give the lady the warmer fire, Pike," Whiskey Sam said.

"Sam, I didn't know you were such a gentleman. The lady and I plan to do some talking into the night and we don't want to keep you awake."

"Continuing with the lessons, huh?" McConnell asked.

"What else can we do with you three around all the time?" Pike asked, and Liz blushed, an odd reaction, considering where she had been working only a day ago.

"All right," McConnell said. "We'll leave you two alone."

Pike and Liz talked until late and then went to sleep. Pike was surprised at how much of what he told Liz she was able to retain.

In the morning she prepared breakfast for them, and again the men appreciated the meal. Pike had decided that even if the food tasted the same, just the fact that a woman—a good-looking woman—had prepared it made it better for them.

He watched her as she ate, and liked the way she looked without any of the makeup she had worn in her previous job. Her face was scrubbed clean, and most whores did not look quite so good in this condition. She looked at least as good as when she was all fixed up.

"We moving on early?" McConnell asked.

"I want to get some idea of how she shoots, first," Pike said. "You fellas can move on, we'll catch up."

"We'll camp for lunch and wait for you," McConnell said. "Maybe we'll bag a buffalo while you're back here playing games."

"Sure," Pike said. "Take all the mules."

When McConnell, Whiskey Sam and Dick Post were mounted up, all Pike and Liz had were their horses and gear to worry about. They'd be able to catch up to the others fairly easily because they were less burdened.

"See you in a few hours," McConnell said.

"You got the right fella teaching you how to shoot, Liz," Whiskey Sam said. "Pike is the best shot either side of the Rockies."

"That's good to know, Sam," Liz said. "Thanks."

They watched the three men until they disappeared from sight and then Liz said, "Now that they're gone, shall we lie down in the snow?"

"Hell, no," Pike said.

"Why not?" she asked, bristling for a moment.

"We told them we were going to shoot," Pike said, "and that's just what we're going to do. Besides, if you and I were to lie down in the snow we'd drown."

"In snow?"

"It wouldn't stay snow once we got started, Liz," he said, smiling.

She finally understood and smiled.

"All right," he said. He picked up her rifle and handed it to her. "Shoot something."

"What?"

"Anything. I just want to see how you hold the rifle . . ."

She took the rifle from him, turned toward a snowbank and shouldered the weapon.

"Go ahead, fire," he said when she looked at him.

She smiled and pulled the trigger, then staggered from the kick.

"You've got to set yourself so that the recoil doesn't knock you off balance," he said. "Try again."

She shouldered the weapon again. He was impressed by the way she steadied the weapon. It was a large, cumbersome thing for a woman, but she was a large woman, stronger than most.

"Wait," he said. He moved to her and smacked her thighs until her legs were set to his satisfaction. After that he straightened her back and squared her shoulders.

"This is not comfortable," she said.

"It may not be comfortable," he said, "but it's correct. Now fire again."

She aimed at the snowbank again and fired. She handled the recoil better this time and turned to

76

him, pleased.

"I hit it," she said.

"You hit it," he said, shaking his head. "It's a snowbank, for godsake. When you can hit the snowflake I want you to hit, then you can look proud."

Her face fell. She pouted at him and she said, "Are you going to be a mean teacher?"

He grinned tightly at her and said, "I'm going to be a tough teacher."

Chapter Twelve

The Blackfoot brave known as Tall Bear watched the man and woman as they worked with the rifle.

The woman apparently knew almost nothing about firing the weapon, and it puzzled Tall Bear that the man was bothering to try to teach her. Tall Bear had seen the woman prepare breakfast for the four men, and wondered what more they could want of her. Naturally, she would belong to one of them, and Tall Bear assumed that it was the biggest of the men, the man who was now showing her how to shoot.

Tall Bear knew how to shoot. He was one of Strong Wolf's men—in fact, he was Strong Wolf's right arm, and Strong Wolf made certain that his braves knew how to use the white man's weapons. Tall Bear was not carrying the white man's weapon now. In fact he carried no weapon now but his knife. It was all he would need, even if the four white men saw him. He was, after all, one of Strong Wolf's men.

The large white man seemed to know a lot about

firing the weapon, although he had not yet fired it himself. Tall Bear wondered why not. Wouldn't it have been better to *show* the woman how it was done?

Tall Bear continued to watch, because that was all Strong Wolf had told him to do. He would have preferred to move down among them while they were asleep and slit one of their throats. He laughed to himself at what the faces of the others would have looked like when they woke the next morning and found one of their number dead like that.

Or he could have sneaked down and taken their woman. From what he could see of her—she was covered from head to foot with clothes—she seemed to be very solidly built. She'd make a fine squaw.

Perhaps later, Strong Wolf would let him have her—after he had killed her man.

Chapter Thirteen

Pike and Liz caught up to the other three while they were camping for lunch.

"Dried meat," Whiskey Sam was complaining. "We brung a woman along and we're having dried meat for lunch."

"I didn't come along just to cook, Sam," Liz told him.

Sam looked up at her and saw that he had insulted her.

"Uh, I'm sorry," he said, lamely.

She smiled at him then and said, "No, that's all right, Sam."

She and Pike dismounted.

"You can hardly help yourself," she added. "After all, at your age, what else would you need a woman for?"

Sam nodded, then, realizing what she had said, looked at her and said, "What?"

The others began to laugh and Liz said, "I'll make

the coffee."

"We've got company," Pike said, over coffee.

"Company?" McConnell asked.

"Who?" Liz said.

"A Blackfoot brave."

"An Indian?" she asked. She was about to look around when Pike said, "No, don't look for him, Liz. You wouldn't see him."

"And you can?" she asked.

"Not now," he said, "but I've seen him."

"Just one?" Whiskey Sam asked.

"One's enough," Pike said. "After all, he's just watching us."

"For what?" Liz asked.

"Maybe he likes you," Pike said.

"Be serious."

"I am."

She swallowed, looked at him and said, "You are?"

He looked at her and said soothingly, "Only partly."

"Somehow, that doesn't make me feel a whole lot better," she said.

"Don't worry about it," Pike told her. "So far he's just watching us."

"How long has he been there?" she asked.

"I spotted him this morning watching us work with the rifle," Pike said, "but I'd be willing to bet he's been with us longer than that."

"You mean he could have sneaked down on us and murdered us in our sleep?" Liz asked.

"Naw," McConnell said, "he'd have no reason to

do that."

She breathed easier—until Whiskey Sam said, "Oh yeah, well I've known some young bucks who'd do that just for the practice."

Liz stared at him in horror while McConnell gave the older man a warning look.

"Hey—" Sam said, shrugging his shoulders helplessly.

"Drink your coffee, Sam," Pike said. "I'm going to take a walk."

"I'll come with you," McConnell said.

"But—" Liz said, half rising. Pike settled her back with a wave of his hand.

Pike and McConnell walked out of earshot of the others.

"What do you think?" McConnell asked.

"Could be just a curious brave."

"You believe that?"

Pike looked at McConnell and shrugged.

"What about your dream?"

"What about it?"

"You didn't have it last night, did you?"

"No."

"Well, maybe—"

"Maybe what?" Pike asked. "Maybe it's going to come true? We can't assume that simply because of the appearance of one lone Blackfoot brave. Besides, there's been no signs of a grizzly around."

"So, what do we do?"

"Nothing," Pike said. "We continue with our hunt—and keep Whiskey Sam from scaring the lady."

"Oh, I don't know," McConnell said. "She got

him pretty good with that shot about men his age."

"Yeah," Pike said, laughing at the thought, "she did, didn't she?"

After lunch they mounted up and started off again, all together. Just once Pike had caught a glimpse of the Blackfoot brave watching them from a ridge.

"Is he still there?" Liz asked.

"He's still there."

"Doing what?"

"He's just watching."

"Pike, what do Indians do to white women?"

He looked over at her.

"Honestly?"

"Honestly."

"Some of them they kill; some of them they take as squaws."

"Um, which do they kill and which do they take as squaws?"

He smiled at her and said, "They kill the weak, skinny ones and the strong, meaty ones they take as squaws."

"Meaty?"

"They feel that they can do the work the weak ones can't, and they'll also make good child-bearers." He made a show of looking her over and said, "I don't think you have anything to worry about."

"About being killed," she asked, "or being taken as a squaw?"   .

Pike smiled.

Chapter Fourteen

The grizzly raised his huge head and sniffed the cold air tentatively. Of all the animal's senses smell was its most acute, while it weakest was vision. This particular grizzly tested the air several times without being able to identify the new scent it was picking up. It was used to smelling puma, buffalo and other animals it shared the region with, and although it could not differentiate between Indians and white men, it was used to the smell of Indians.

The smell of white men was new to it, and so the scent was confusing.

The normal grizzly will measure some eighty inches in length and weigh as much as five hundred pounds. This was not, however, a normal grizzly. Oh, it had the coarse, thick brown hair usual to its species, the small eyes and ears, the typically short neck and large, doglike head, but this animal exceeded the more usual length and weight classifications by little less than half again in length and twice that in weight.

Now, although confused by this new scent, it was not particularly worried, or threatened. The grizzly bear is, by nature, a gentle animal, although it did have a reputation for being ferocious. In truth, it became so only when threatened, or wounded. Under those situations the animal killed easily and swiftly, due to its tremendous strength and huge claws and teeth.

This grizzly tested the air again and then went back to its hunt for food. The bear usually ate vegetation, although it would eat meat if it came upon already dead game, perhaps left behind by the puma. This bear, however, had found neither in some time—at least, not enough to satisfy its huge appetite—and now gave all its attention to finding food. That was all it was interested in.

At the moment.

Chapter Fifteen

"Sweet Jesus," Whiskey Sam said.

"What is it?" McConnell asked. Pike and Liz were too far back to have heard the old man's words.

Whiskey Sam dismounted now and McConnell saw what had shocked him so. The older man was crouched over some tracks in the snow.

Tracks made by a bear.

"What's happening?" Pike asked, riding up next to McConnell.

McConnell, at a loss for words, watched his friend's face and saw the look on it when Pike recognized the tracks.

"Sam?" Pike said.

Whiskey Sam looked up at them, his hand still resting in the center of one of the animal's tracks.

"Grizzly," he said, "and by the looks of these tracks, the biggest damned grizzly I've ever seen."

. . . For a moment Pike saw the grizzly in his dream, standing up on its hind legs, almost blocking out the sky . . .

"How big, Sam?" he asked.

"Jesus," Sam said, "this is a monster, Pike. I mean, I've seen some big grizzlies in my time. Saw Jim Bridger kill one that was damn near seven hundred pounds once, but this . . . this one makes that one look like a cub."

"Oh my . . ." Liz breathed. "I've never seen a grizzly."

"Gentle as lambs, ma'am," Sam said, finally standing up, "less'n you rile 'em." He looked down at the tracks again and said, "Sure would like to see this one."

"We're looking for buffalo, Sam," Pike reminded him.

Sam looked up at Pike, hearing something in his voice.

"That don't mean we can't go after a grizzly if we see it," Sam said. "Biggest damn grizzly I ever seen was that one Bridger killed, and it took two shots and a bowie knife before a head shot finally put that one down. The man who kills this brizzly would be a legend."

"There's enough legends in the world now," Pike said. "Come on, let's hunt buffalo."

Pike rode ahead as Whiskey Sam mounted his horse and looked at McConnell.

"What's wrong with him?"

McConnell shrugged.

"Guess he don't like grizzlies. Come on, let's hunt buffalo."

"He almost looked like he was . . . afraid," Whiskey Sam said, refusing to let it go.

"Pike's not afraid of anything, Sam," McConnell

88

said, and urged his horse on.

Looking after him, Whiskey Sam said, "That's what I always thought."

When they camped for the night Pike was obviously preoccupied. McConnell knew what he was thinking. Liz was along, there was a Blackfoot dogging their trail, and now evidence of a grizzly. All of the parts of the dream were coming together.

McConnell was also aware of the way Whiskey Sam and Dick Post were looking at Pike. Obviously, Sam had spoken to Dick about what he was thinking.

Liz was very quiet. She cooked, she sat next to Pike and ate, watching him, and then she cleaned up.

There was a lot of tension in the air.

"Pike?"

Piked started and looked at McConnell.

"We don't need all this tension."

"What tension?" Pike asked.

"Sam's a little worried about the way you reacted to those bear tracks back there."

Pike looked at Sam.

"That so, Sam?"

Looking nervous, Sam said, "I was just thinking out loud."

Pike looked at McConnell, who nodded.

"All right," Pike said. "I guess you got a right to know what's eating me."

Whiskey Sam and Dick Post listened intently while Pike related his dream to them.

"You got to talk to an Indian—" Whiskey Sam started to say, but Pike cut him off.

"I already talked to Ted Clark's woman, Sky Woman," Pike said. "She couldn't help. She just said I'd have to wait."

"Well," Sam said, "we could go back."

"No," Pike said, "that's not the way. I figure to see it through. None of you have to come with me, though."

Sam and Dick exchanged glances, and Sam said, "We'll stick."

Pike didn't have to look at McConnell and Liz to know that they were staying.

"I appreciate it."

"Pike," Whiskey Sam said, "I'm sorry—"

Pike held up his hand to ward off his friend's apology.

"No need, Sam," Pike said. "You got a right to think what you want. I didn't give you much choice, until now."

"With that Indian lurking around," McConnell said, "how about we set some watches?"

"Good idea," Pike said. "I'll take the first."

"I'll take the second," McConnell said.

Sam and Dick took the third and fourth. They decided Liz wouldn't have to take a watch.

"Just be up bright and early to make breakfast," Sam said.

"Sam," she said, "I can see why you're not married."

"Never found a woman who would have me," the old man said.

She smiled and said, "That's what I figured."

✿   ✿   ✿

When the dream came it was Liz, lying next to him, who heard him first, and not McConnell, who was on watch.

She rolled over and put her hand over his mouth. "Pike!" she hissed.

He came awake, aware that she was there. She had awakened him before he could find out much more about the dream—but at least she'd awakened him before he could wake anyone else up.

"Are you all right?"

"Yes," he said, easing her hand down from his mouth. "What was I doing?"

"Not much, just breathing hard and sweating."

"How'd you know—"

"I've been watching you."

"What?"

"Keeping an eye on you."

"You haven't slept?"

"I haven't been able to," she said, moving closer to him. They were far enough from the two still sleeping men so that they could not be heard. "I've been lying here wanting your hands on me, wanting you inside me . . ."

"Liz . . ." he said warningly as she put her hand on the front of his pants.

"They won't hear."

"Skins . . ."

"He won't hear."

"You aren't exactly quiet about it, you know," he reminded her.

"I'll just use my mouth," she whispered in his ear. "I want you—"

"It's cold!"

91

"I'll keep it warm," she promised, undoing the front of his pants.

"Jesus," he said when he felt her fingers on him.

In the dark she moved her head down. This isn't right, he thought, as the cold air hit his penis ... Then her mouth came down over him like a hot towel, her hand gripped him at the base. She wished she could get at his balls, but they were buried inside his pants.

She worked her mouth over him wetly and he lifted his hips to her, feeling the rush in his loins. As she suckled him he wondered if he was going to be able to keep quiet when he exploded into her mouth.

He could hear her making little wet sounds as her head went up and down, and he hoped the others couldn't hear it. Where was McConnell, he wondered. What was he doing?

Finally he couldn't hold it back and he ejaculated into her mouth. She accommodated his entire emission without a sound, and he was able to keep his own reaction down to a dull roar. Of course, to him it sounded as if they were making enough noise to wake the entire mountain.

She tucked him back away inside his pants and then moved next to him.

"Now go to sleep," he said.

"Now I'll be able to," she said, happily.

She didn't fool him. She didn't need sex that badly, but she had accomplished what she'd set out to.

For a little while, he had forgotten all about the dream.

Chapter Sixteen

Pike woke before Dick Post could wake him. He started breakfast without waking Liz. It was his way of paying her back for what she'd done for him during the night—well, not so much *what* she'd done as *why*.

Dick Post mosied over for the first cup of coffee out of the pot, and Pike took the second. They drank while the pan heated on the fire.

"Gonna wake them?"

"The smell should be waking them pretty soon," Post replied, sitting next to Pike. "Pike, I think I should tell you why I agreed to come on this hunt when Whiskey Sam invited me."

"Okay," Pike said, "so tell me."

"I've heard a lot about you over the years," Post said, "especially over the past few years. They've started mentioning your name in the same breath as Bridger's."

"Who is they?"

"Oh, you know," Post said, shrugging, "hunters

93

and trappers talking around a campfire."

"And you wanted to see if I was worthy of that mention?"

"I wanted to meet you, see what you were like," Post said. "I hope there's nothing wrong with that."

Now Pike shrugged.

"Nothing wrong with being curious, Dick. Happens to most everybody at one time or another."

"I appreciate that."

"I suppose this dream business has dampened your enthusiasm a little."

"No, not at all," Post said. "You see, a few years ago I had a recurring dream."

"You did?"

Post nodded.

"For about two weeks I had the same dream most every night," Post said.

"What was it about?"

"Dying."

"Your own death?"

Post nodded.

"What happened?"

"It stopped coming."

"Just like that?"

"Just like that."

"Do you mind if I ask . . ."

"How I died in my dream?"

"Did you . . . actually die?"

"Well, no, I always woke up before . . . before that." Pike could see that the man was still affected by the dream. "In my dream I was hunting buffalo— just like now—and there was a lot of snow. As I was trying to set up for a shot at a big bull the snow suddenly went out from under me, like it was just a thin layer over a hole—like a trap. In the dream I'm falling, falling a long way . . . and I always woke up before I hit bottom."

"Chilling," Pike said, meaning no pun.

"Yes, it was," Post said, "just like yours probably is."

They sat in silence for a few moments, sipping their coffee, and then Pike tossed some bacon into the pan. Soon, the aroma of frying bacon mingled with that of coffee started waking the others.

Whiskey Sam woke first, rubbing the sleep vigorously from his face with a couple of handfuls of snow.

"Gimme a cup of that coffee," he said, and accepted it from Pike. He drank it scalding hot.

"Jesus," Pike said, "how can you do that without peeling your lips off?"

Whiskey Sam smiled and said, "Years and years of practice."

McConnell and Liz woke next and accepted a cup of coffee each.

"I'm supposed to be the first one up, to start breakfast," Liz said, looking at Pike.

"I was up," he said, and that was the only reason he gave the others. He and she knew the real reason.

"Liz, put your hat on," Pike instructed.

"Why?" she asked. She had been running her hands through her long, dark hair.

"With that Blackfoot watching, we don't want to advertise the fact that we've got a woman with us," McConnell said.

"At least," Whiskey Sam added, "not one that

95

looks like you."

Hurriedly, she grabbed her hat and tucked her hair up underneath it.

McConnell gave Pike a searching look, trying to figure out whether or not he'd had the dream. Pike wondered if he should start lying about it, so that the others wouldn't be thinking—and asking—about it every morning.

After breakfast Liz insisted on being the one to clean up. While she did that the men saddled the horses and packed up the supplies.

The conversation with Dick Post had made Pike feel much better about his dream. He still couldn't figure it out, or stop being confused and worried about it, but at least he knew he wasn't alone. At least he knew that there were other people who had dreams like that.

At least he knew he wasn't going mad.

Pike helped Liz mount up and appreciated the fact that she didn't ask him how he was. He didn't need to be babied by her or by the others.

"All right, people," he said when they were all mounted and ready to go, "we're going to find us some buffalo today. I can feel it!"

"I hope so," Liz said, smiling at him. "I'm tired of shooting at snow."

Chapter Seventeen

Tall Bear wanted the woman.

He had crept closer to them in the night, taking care not to be seen by their sentry, and he had seen what the woman had done to the big man. It had inflamed Tall Bear's desire. Now more than anything he wanted to kill all the men and take the woman for his own use.

He had never seen a squaw do what the white woman had done with her mouth.

In the morning Tall Bear had moved back to higher ground and watched the woman run her hands through her black hair. Indian women had such straight hair, but this woman's hair had waves in it, and hung past her shoulders, still. He was wetting his lips when she tucked her hair up beneath her hat, and then he cursed.

Behind him he heard a noise, but knew that it was only his comrades, finally catching up.

He turned and saw his friend, Fear Bringer. Fear Bringer was larger than Tall Bear, which made him a very big man, indeed. Tall Bear knew that if Fear Bringer saw the woman and decided that he wanted her, then he himself would never be able to have her. But he also knew that Fear Bringer preferred fighting and killing to taking women, so he felt sure that his claim would be safe.

Tall Bear watched now as Fear Bringer approached him, dismounting and leaving the other ten braves mounted and waiting. The bigger man had muscles in his arms like rocks, a chest like slabs of stone, legs like tree trunks. His hands were huge, capable of crushing a man's skull. When they were very young Tall Bear had seen the wisdom of becoming best friends with Fear Bringer, and over the years it had paid off more than once.

In addition to being very large, Fear Bringer was also very handsome. Although he had been in many fights as a child, his great size had kept him from sustaining any damage, such as a broken nose or a scar. No, it was Fear Bringer who inflicted damage on others, and retained the handsome visage which made him a prime catch for the young squaws in their village—if he were interested in taking a wife.

"How many are there, little brother?" Fear Bringer asked, joining his friend.

Though the same age, Fear Bringer had always been larger than Tall Bear, and from a very early age had taken to calling him "little brother."

"Four men and a woman."

"A woman?" Fear Bringer said, raising his eyebrows. "Is she pleasing to you?"

"Very much."

"Then you shall have her," Fear Bringer said,

clapping his friend on the shoulder with force enough to make the smaller man wince.

As a child the larger man had been called Little Buffalo until he had begun to grow more rapidly than the others his age. When it came time to take his manhood name, Fear Bringer seemed a natural name for him, for his size always struck fear into the hearts of his enemies—and some of his friends.

"Is there a white man worthy of me?" Fear Bringer asked now.

"Yes," Tall Bear said.

He was pleased that the woman's man was such a big man. Now she would be able to watch while Fear Bringer brought her man to his knees.

"See the large one?" he said, pointing. "Wait, he stands—see?"

"Aieee!" Fear Bringer said, reacting the way most braves did when they saw a particularly pleasing squaw, a huge buffalo, or a handsome pony. "He is the largest white man I have ever seen—and look at those shoulders!"

"He will be a fine challenge for you, Fear Bringer," Tall Bear said. "He is almost as big as you are."

"That is good, little brother," Fear Bringer said, his pleasure plain in his voice. "I have not had a worthy opponent in a long time."

Tall Bear hoped for a moment that the white man would not be *too* worthy. Ahh, he thought then, no white man could ever humble Fear Bringer.

Not even a white man this size.

Chapter Eighteen

At midday they found a small herd of buffalo.

"What do we do?" Liz asked, looking down at the dozen or so animals. "Sit up here and shoot them?"

"Well, we could," McConnell said.

"That doesn't sound fair."

"We could also ride down there and each pick one out," Whiskey Sam said.

"And then what?" she asked.

"And then ride him down," Pike said. "The animal has a fair chance of getting away, that way."

"That sounds . . . dangerous."

"It would be more dangerous with a larger herd," Dick Post said. "Then there would be more of a chance of you falling off your horse and being trampled."

Liz made a face.

"There aren't enough of them for all of us to ride down there," McConnell observed. "They'd scatter before we even got among 'em."

"One of us goes, then," Whiskey Sam said. "That

way, we're sure of getting one."

"How can you be sure you'll get one?" Liz asked.

Whiskey Sam gave her a gapped smile and said, "Because Pike will be the one to go down. He don't miss."

She looked at Pike and said, "Really?"

Pike shrugged.

"Are we agreed that Pike will go?" McConnell asked.

Sam nodded, as did Dick Post.

"All right, girl," Whiskey Sam said. "Now we'll sit up here and you'll see how it's done."

Pike handed his Hawken to McConnell and began to ease his horse down the slope toward the buffalo.

"How is he going to shoot a buffalo without his rifle?" she asked.

"Since he'll be riding the animal down," McConnell said, "he won't be able to shoulder his rifle, so he'll have to use his pistol."

"Will a pistol down an animal that size?" she asked.

"If Pike puts his ball in the right place," Whiskey Sam replied.

"And he only gets one try," Dick Post said.

"Even with a small herd, this sounds dangerous," Liz said, looking worried.

"It is," McConnell said, and they all settled back to watch.

After Pike had descended the slope he began walking his horse toward the herd. At one point one of the animals lifted his head and, figuring that he had finally been noticed, Pike kicked his horse in the side and they started to gallop.

Alerted now, the buffalo began to run, a slow, rolling gait. It took longer for the buffalo to accelerate than it did for Pike's horse. Pike picked out a big bull and began to run toward him. To do so he had to ride into the center of the herd.

"If he falls—" Liz said, putting her hands to her mouth.

"Pike don't fall," Whiskey Sam said, obviously deriving pleasure from what he was watching.

They watched as Pike's horse gradually closed the distance between man and buffalo, until finally Pike was right next to the animal. He drew his pistol.

"Bad," Whiskey Sam said.

"What?" Liz asked.

"Pike wasn't able to get on the left side of the animal," Sam said. "The others forced him to the right."

"What's wrong with that?"

McConnell explained.

"Pike is right-handed. He'll now have to fire across his body."

"Can he—"

"Shh," Whiskey Sam said. "Watch!"

They did just that as Pike reached across his body with his pistol, found the spot he wanted and fired.

For a moment Liz thought he had missed completely, but then the running buffalo missed a step, then seemed to stagger. Pike rode past the animal, maneuvered himself away from the rest of the herd and rode back.

The stricken animal had stopped, and Liz thought it was waiting for Pike to return, to go after him.

Pike stopped his horse a few yards from the buffalo

103

and dismounted.

"Why is he getting down?" she asked. "He hasn't reloaded!"

"He doesn't have time," Whiskey Sam said. "He'll have to finish it with his knife."

"Kill a buffalo with a knife?" Liz asked, shocked.

"Watch, Liz," McConnell said.

They were not the only ones watching, however.

"The big man has courage," Fear Bringer said.

"And skill," Tall Bear said.

"Even better," Fear Bringer said.

Tall Bear, Fear Bringer and the other ten braves were all watching Pike stalk and kill the buffalo.

"Should we go down now?" Fear Bringer asked.

"Let us wait until he has begun skinning the animal," Tall Bear said. "Then we will go down and take it from them."

"And kill them?" Fear Bringer asked.

"No," Tall Bear said, "not yet."

Pike had not approached the animal, although he did now have his knife out. She watched as it seemed Pike and the animal were watching each other very carefully. Suddenly, the animal just keeled over and fell heavily to the ground.

"Oh, God . . ." she said, breathing a sigh of relief.

Now Pike ran forward and knelt by the animal, found his spot and drove the knife in to the hilt. The animal shuddered once, and lay still.

"It wasn't dead?" she asked.

104

"Not until Pike put his knife into him," Whiskey Sam said. "Come on, let's go on down."

They all rode down the slope and, as they approached Pike, he had already begun skinning the animal.

"That was wonderful," Liz cried out, starting to dismount.

She was surprised when Pike sprang to his feet, ran to her and pushed her back into the saddle.

"What the—" she said.

"Look!" Pike cried out.

They all turned and looked behind them and saw the dozen or so Indians riding down the slope toward them.

"Jesus," McConnell said.

"Christ!" Whiskey Sam said. "We finally got one and now these heathens are gonna take it away from us."

As Pike ran to his horse and mounted, McConnell said, "Yeah . . . if we're lucky they'll stop for it!"

Chapter Nineteen

As they started to run, Pike waited until Liz was ahead of him, and took off after her. As they rode, he looked back at the Blackfoot braves and saw that they had stopped at the corpse of the buffalo—all but one. He continued on, as if to keep track of them. Briefly, Pike considered trying to hide along the way and take care of the brave, but he decided against it.

He quickened his horse's pace and drew up alongside McConnell.

"They're not chasing us," he called out. "Just one brave, to keep track of us."

"Want to take care of him?"

Pike shook his head.

"They've started playing a game with us," Pike said. "If they wanted us dead, they could run us down fairly easily, with these mules slowing us down."

"So what's the game?" McConnell asked.

"Let's think about that after we put some space between them and us," Pike suggested.

They rode hard for over an hour then decided to

give the horses a rest.

"Why didn't they come after us?" Liz asked.

"They're obviously playing some kind of a game with us," Whiskey Sam said.

"That's what we figured," McConnell said.

"What kind of a game?" Liz asked.

"Well, they've taken a fresh kill from us," Pike said. "Maybe they plan to do that to us for as long as we're up here hunting."

"But . . . why?" she asked.

"Who knows?" Whiskey Sam said. "Maybe they're bored."

"So they won't try to kill us?" Liz asked, hopefully. "They'll just keep stealing dead buffalo from us?"

"Not necessarily," McConnell said.

"No," Whiskey Sam said, "they'll keep stealing our kills until they get bored with that and then they'll try and kill us."

Whiskey Sam wondered why he was getting dirty looks from Pike and McConnell.

They moved on again, at a slower pace this time.

"Pike?" Liz said.

"Yes?"

"If we know they're going to keep stealing our . . . our kills, why don't we just give it up and go back down the mountain to the settlement?"

"For one thing, to go back we'd have to get past them. It's better to keep going. We'll come to another settlement eventually."

"What if they decide to kill us?"

"Well, then we'll either have to run, or fight . . . or hide."

"With these mules?"

"No, we'll have to cut the mules loose. That'll be another plus for them."

"And me?" she asked, recalling stories she'd heard about Indians and white women.

"Let's not start worrying about something before it's time, okay?" he said. "Very likely we're finished with them altogether."

"I hope so," she said, totally unaware that there was still a Blackfoot brave on their trail.

Pike was aware of it, though.

Only too aware.

"We've still got somebody on our trail," McConnell said.

They had stopped for a simple lunch of dried meat and water. They didn't want to take a chance on settling in. Not yet, anyway.

"I know," Pike said.

"As long as they always know where we are, we might as well forget the hunt and head for the nearest settlement."

"The nearest settlement is Clark's Fork," Pike reminded him, "and to get there we've got to get past them."

"What's the next settlement we'll come to if we keep going?" McConnell asked.

Whiskey Sam heard the question.

"That'd be Remsen's Junction," he said.

"How far?" McConnell asked.

"Seventy miles, maybe more."

"A day and a half's ride on the flat," Pike said. "Up here three days, and with the mules closer to five."

McConnell scratched his chin and said, "Jesus, we might as well keep hunting and see what happens."

"I agree," Whiskey Sam said.

"There's one other possibility," Pike said.

"What's that?"

"They may be waiting for more braves."

"How many did you count?" McConnell asked.

"About twelve," Pike said. "Sam?"

"Yeah, about that."

At that point Liz and Post came over.

"Ready to go?" Post asked. He'd known that the other three were probably discussing the situation, so he'd made sure he kept Liz occupied.

"Yeah, we might as well keep moving. Maybe we can track that herd," Pike said.

"While the Indians are tracking us," Liz said wryly, showing them all that she was no fool.

PART THREE

THE CHASE

Chapter Twenty

There were no further incidents with the Blackfoot Indians the rest of the day. That evening they decided to go ahead and chance making a fire and cooking a hot meal. They didn't think the Indians would come after them at night.

"Because Indians don't attack at night?" Liz asked.

"No," Pike said, "because that would end the game too quickly."

"Indians play games?" she asked.

"All the time," Pike said. "It's how they test your courage. Courage is very important to Indians."

"That's comforting," she said. "What do they do after they test your courage?"

"If you fail, they kill you," Pike said.

"And if you pass?"

"Sometimes they kill you, anyway," Whiskey Sam said, ever the optimist.

"Sam," Pike said.

"What?"

"Take the first watch."

"Why do I have to take the first watch?"

"Because," McConnell said, "you're old and it'll give you more uninterrupted sleep than the rest of us."

Grumbling, "I could get that by taking the last watch," Whiskey Sam rose, picked up his rifle and went to keep watch.

"I like him," Liz said.

"He likes you, too," Dick Post said. "Otherwise he wouldn't talk to you at all."

"Maybe you'd be better off," Skins McConnell said, "if he didn't like you."

Pike took the last watch and, as first light dawned, he decided to stroll out a little farther and see what he could see. He was mildly pleased that he had slept without experiencing the dream—or he had dreamed and did not remember it. Either one was preferable to what had been going on for the past couple of weeks.

He was walking rather aimlessly until he saw something in the snow that attracted his attention. He went over, looked at it, and what he saw didn't please him.

He went back and woke the rest of them up.

"We had company during the night," he said.

"When?" McConnell asked.

"Hard to tell, but there's footprints in the snow."

"Bear?" Whiskey Sam asked.

Pike shook his head.

"Indian."

"You mean . . . they came in close to our camp?" Liz asked.

114

"Yeah, looks that way," Pike said.

"Even though we had watch posted?"

Pike nodded.

"Nobody moves like an Indian, Liz," he said.

"We could have been killed in our sleep!"

"No," Pike said, "they wouldn't have been able to get that close—not without killing whoever was on watch, that is."

"Then how close did they get?"

"Just close enough to get some idea of what they were dealing with."

"Just close enough," Whiskey Sam said, "for a good smell."

They started to pack up, Pike and McConnell taking care of the mules.

"You know they're eventually going to want these mules," McConnell said.

"I know," Pike said. "It's just a matter of time."

"Maybe we should try leaving them something after we camp," McConnell said.

"You think they're going to be satisfied with that?" Pike asked.

"Satisfied, no, but it might prolong the game."

"I don't want to prolong the game, Skins," Pike said. "If they're going to come for us I'd rather it be sooner than later."

"Yeah," McConnell said, "I know what you mean."

When the mules were ready they all mounted. Pike risked a look behind them and spotted one lone Indian up on a ridge.

One thing about hunting in the mountains, he thought. No matter how high you are, somebody can get up higher.

After they had been riding a while Liz said, "Pike?"

"Yes?"

"Why don't we just run for it?" she asked. "I mean, just leave the mules and the supplies behind and run for it."

"We can't."

"Wouldn't that satisfy them?"

"We can't run, Liz—"

"We ran before!"

"That's because someone was chasing us," he explained. "I told you how much stock they place in courage. If we ran now—right now, when there's no immediate danger—they'd take that as a sign of cowardice."

"Well," she said, sarcastically, "God forbid we should be cowards—live cowards."

"We wouldn't be live cowards, Liz," Pike said, "we'd be dead ones."

They rode in silence for a while and then she turned to him. She reached out to put her hand on his arm, but they were too far apart for that.

"I'm sorry," she said.

"There's nothing to be sorry about," he told her.

"I'm afraid."

"Well, that's sure not something to be sorry about," he said. "Hell, I'm afraid."

"Are you really?" she asked, looking surprised.

"You don't show it."

"Honey, that's the trick," he said, "not to show it—to *them!*"

She chanced a look behind them and then said, "I'll try, Pike. I really will."

"You've been doing fine, Liz," he said. "Just fine."

For the first time he wished he'd left her behind in that whorehouse.

"What have we got, Sam?" Pike asked. They had stopped and Pike rode up to see what the holdup was.

"More tracks," Sam said, pointing to the ground.

Pike looked and saw the huge bearpaw tracks ahead of them in the snow.

"Same one?" he asked.

"Jesus," Sam said, "I'd hate to think that there were two grizzlies up here that size."

"Well, we're crossing his tracks," Pike said. "He's not going in our direction."

"That don't make no nevermind," Sam said. "This baby goes anywhere he wants anytime he wants."

"Maybe he'll double back and give our friends the Blackfoot a scare," Dick Post offered.

"Them crazy Indians would take a bear this size as a challenge," Whiskey Sam said, then added, "That is, if they don't take him for some kind of god."

"A god?" Liz said, riding up alongside them. "Who's a god?"

"Indians often believe that animals are infused with the spirits of gods—usually a wolf, or a big cat."

"A bear this size," Whiskey Sam said, "even I'm

117

tempted to think he's some kind of a god."

Liz looked at Sam to see if he was kidding, and couldn't tell.

They all sat there for a few moments, silently gazing down at the tracks.

"We'd better get moving," Pike said. "The faster we do, the faster our friends will reach this point and see the tracks. Then they can decide what they want to do about it."

"Maybe they'll forget about us," Liz said, hopefully.

"Yeah," Pike said without much hope, "maybe."

Chapter Twenty-one

When the Blackfoot braves reached the tracks they stopped short and stared. The only one who didn't look surprised was Tall Bear. He had seen the tracks earlier.

"Again," he said.

"You have seen these before?" Fear Bringer asked.

"Yes."

"Have you see the animal they belong to?"

"Not yet."

"He must be magnificent," Fear Bringer said. "A bear of such size, he must be a god."

Tall Bear looked at his friend and remembered that from a very young age Fear Bringer had been very superstitious. Tall Bear, on the other hand, had never been superstitious.

"You do not think so?" Fear Bringer asked, noticing the look Tall Bear was giving him.

"It is a bear, my friend," Tall Bear said. "That is all."

"Perhaps," Fear Bringer said, "but such a bear!"

He looked at his friend and said, "You took your name from a bear. You of all people should know—"

"I took the name because he is strong," Tall Bear said, cutting the bigger man off. "That is the only reason."

"We will see who is right when we find this bear."

"We are not looking for the bear," Tall Bear said. "We are following the whites."

"We will all come together," Fear Bringer said with certainty. "You will see."

Chapter Twenty-two

The bear was starting to feel crowded.

He could smell the Indians, the white men, the horses, the mules, and they all made him feel jumpy. On top of that, he had a powerful hunger he could not quite satisfy. The jumble of scents, the rumbling of his stomach and the confusion in his brain were combining to make him a very irritable creature.

It was a big mountain, but the bear was starting to feel crowded.

Chapter Twenty-three

Eventually they encountered another small herd of buffalo. They couldn't tell whether it was the same herd or not, but that didn't matter.

"How are we going to do it this time?" McConnell said.

"Let's find some high ground downwind from them and take our shots," Pike said. "Maybe we'll have time to take some skin and meat and get moving before the Indians come upon us again."

"And then?" McConnell asked.

"And then we'll keep going and look for more. Eventually we'll start down and come to another settlement—maybe even a town."

"I told you where the next settlement was—" Whiskey Sam began.

"Maybe another one popped up since the last time you were here, Sam," Pike said. He pinned the old man with a hard stare to keep him from saying anything else.

"Come on, Liz," he said, "you're going to take the first shot?"

"I am?"

"You are."

Once they found the high ground they wanted they dismounted and picketed the animals so they wouldn't spook and run when the shooting started.

"What do I do now?" Liz asked, aware that they were all watching her.

"Aim and fire," Pike said. "Come on, pick out a nice fat one."

Liz studied the herd for a few moments, then raised the rifle to her shoulder, aimed and fired . . .

Pike and Dick Post had had a conversation about Liz taking the first shot earlier on.

"If she misses," Post had complained, "she'll spook 'em and we'll lose 'em."

"Not if you fire right behind her," Pike said.

"She could cost a kill."

"Come on, Post," Pike said. "So, if we miss these we'll get the next ones."

"Yeah, sure . . ." Post said.

"What's the problem?" McConnell had asked, coming up on Pike.

"He's worried about missing a buffalo."

"I guess he doesn't know we came up here to relax as much as to hunt buffalo," McConnell said.

"I guess nobody told him," Pike said. "He's

worried about getting buffalo . . ."

So worried, in fact, that the echo of Liz's shot had not even faded out before Post fired right behind her.

One buffalo keeled over and the others scattered. Pike led one, fired, and watched as the animal lurched, stumbled, and fell. He couldn't see who else fired, but either McConnell or Whiskey Sam downed another one before the herd was gone.

"I got one!" Liz cried out.

"I'm sorry, honey," Dick Poset said, "but you missed. I got him."

She turned to stare at Post, then swiveled her head around to look at Pike for confirmation.

"You missed, Post," Pike said.

"What?"

"I said you missed . . . clean."

"What are you talking about?"

"That buff staggered as soon as Liz's shot hit him. When you fired behind her he was already falling, and your shot missed him clean."

"You don't know what you're talking about," Post said, angrily. "I killed that animal!"

Pike looked at Liz and shook his head.

"Don't do that!" Post snapped.

"What?"

"Don't go making her think she hit that buffalo."

"She did, Post," McConnell said. "I saw it, too."

"What the hell—"

"How many'd we get, Sam?" Pike asked.

"Three," Whiskey Sam said. "Let's stop arguing

125

and get down there to get what we can."

As if in response to his words they suddenly heard the high-pitched cries of Indians.

"Jesus, here they come again," McConnell said.

Off to their right about a dozen Blackfoot braves came over a rise and started riding toward them, yelling at the top of their lungs.

"What do we do?" McConnell asked.

"Do?" Pike said. "None of us have reloaded. What do you think we do?"

"Run!" McConnell said.

"Just as fast as we can."

Liz grabbed his arm and said, "Oh, you mean it's all right to run now?"

They rode as hard as the mules would let them for a while and then Pike called their progress to a halt.

"They did it again," he said, seething. "They chased us off, took our kill and didn't even bother to chase us."

"Did you get a good look at those bucks?" Whiskey Sam asked Pike.

"No, I didn't," Pike said. "Why?"

"'Cause I don't think they did it again."

"What do you mean, they didn't do it again?" McConnell asked. "They came screaming after us—"

"Different Indians," Whiskey Sam said.

"What?" Pike said. "What did you say?"

"Those were different Indians," Whiskey Sam said, "not the same ones."

"Skins?"

"To tell you the truth, I didn't notice."

"Dick?"

"Me neither."

"Jesus, you young fellas are supposed to be the ones with the sharp eyes," Whiskey Sam complained. "Do you remember the last time, there was this big buck out front of them?"

Pike thought back and seemed to remember that one of the Indians was larger than the others.

"That big one wasn't there this time," Whiskey Sam said.

"Maybe he just wasn't there," McConnell offered.

"No," Whiskey Sam said, "they was different Indians."

"That's great," Pike said. "If Sam's right, we've got twice as many Blackfoot to contend with as we did before."

"So what do we do?" Liz said.

"Do?" Pike said. "We get off this goddamned mountain, that's what we do!"

They rode for the remainder of the afternoon until they were hampered by a mule that went lame.

"He's going to hold us back," McConnell said, after examining the animal.

"We'll have to leave it behind," Pike said.

"We should leave them all behind," Post said. "After all, we haven't been able to get anything for them to carry, thanks to the Blackfoot."

"We'll hold on to the others for a while," Pike said.

127

"We *did* pay for them."

"We'll be able to move faster without them," Liz said. She gave Pike a look that said she was just making a suggestion, and not really siding with Post.

"Moving fast is not the key," Pike said. "If they wanted to kill us they could have done it by now. There's only one way we're going to get off this mountain."

"And how's that?" McConnell asked.

Pike looked at them all in turn and then said, "If they let us off."

Chapter Twenty-four

When Tall Bear and Fear Bringer saw the Indians butchering the three dead buffalo they knew two things: They had found the other braves from their group, and those other braves had raided the same group of whites of their kill.

"The whites have gotten past us," Fear Bringer said. He had expected that they would pin the whites between them. His voice revealed his disappointment.

"That is no problem," Tall Bear said. "We will have John Kidd take his men and circle around in front of them. We will trap them between us, and finish them."

"All but that big one," Fear Bringer said. "I want to finish him myself."

Tall Bear smiled and slapped his friend on the shoulders soundly.

"And I want to see it, my friend."

They rode down to the braves who were working over the buffalo, and both Tall Bear and Fear Bringer dismounted and faced John Kidd.

John Kidd had a white man's name because, although he was the same age as the other two, he had not grown up with them. He had been captured when he was young and lived among the whites, and when he had finally rejoined his Blackfoot people he had kept the name to remind him of how much he hated the whites.

John Kidd explained how they had come to take the buffalo from the whites, which verified that it was the same group of whites.

"Four men and a woman," John Kidd said, and Tall Bear nodded.

"When you are finished here," he told John Kidd, "take your braves and circle around. I want you to get in front of them again."

"We will trap them between us?" John Kidd asked.

"Yes."

"Aiee, and then we will crush them."

"And then we will crush them," Tall Bear said.

Tall Bear and Fear Bringer mounted up again, and then Fear Bringer leaned over and asked John Kidd, "Have you seen the bear?"

"I have."

"A huge grizzly of great height?"

"No," John Kidd said, "we saw a grizzly of no great size."

"There is another," Fear Bringer said. "Surely you have seen the tracks."

"I have not," John Kidd said, looking puzzled.

"How is that so?" Fear Bringer asked Tall Bear.

"Perhaps your grizzly god sprouted wings and flew," Tall Bear said, teasing his childhood friend.

130

"Do not scoff."

"The bear is here, Fear Bringer," Tall Bear said. "We will find him for you."

A short time later Tall Bear and Fear Bringer saw the loose mule, and Tall Bear instructed one of his braves to catch it.

"It is lame," the brave said when they reached the point where he was standing with the mule.

"Butcher it," Tall Bear instructed, and they waited while the brave took the choice parts of meat from the carcass.

"They cannot move quickly because of the mules," Fear Bringer said. "Why do they not leave them behind?"

Tall Bear looked at his friend and said, "There is no panic in these whites."

"Who are they led by?"

Tall Bear smiled and said, "The large one."

"So," Fear Bringer said. This made the prospect of meeting such a man in combat even more appealing.

"He will not die easy, that one," Tall Bear said.

"Perhaps not," Fear Bringer said, "but he will die."

Chapter Twenty-five

"What's that?" Liz asked.

They were all looking ahead of them at what appeared to be an animal's carcass.

"Stay here," Pike said, and rode ahead to inspect it.

"It could be a trap," McConnell said to Liz.

"Then why is he riding to it alone?"

"So that if it is a trap, we don't all die," McConnell said.

"Just Pike."

"Pike's a born leader," McConnell said, "and we all know it. Nobody chose him to lead this expedition, but you see who takes charge when something goes wrong."

When he reached it he saw that it was a buffalo, a large but old one. It had apparently been killed with the swipe of a huge bear claw, which had opened its neck to the bone. Since the kill the animal had been gutted by several different scavengers, and there wasn't much left of it—nothing of value, anyway. Even the testicles had been eaten. Around the carcass were more of the huge bear tracks they had been seeing for the past few days.

Pike turned in his saddle and signaled the others to approach.

"What is it?" Liz asked again, as she reached him.

"A dead buffalo," Pike said. "Apparently it was too old to outrun that big grizzly."

"It was the grizzly, all right," Whiskey Sam said. "And he's killed now. He must have been real hungry to go after another animal. They don't usually eat meat unless it's already been killed."

"And to attack an animal this large," McConnell said. "That's really unusual."

"Well, this confirms what we've suspected all along," Pike said.

"What's that?" Liz asked.

"This is not an ordinary grizzly."

They had not stopped for lunch, so when they stopped for dinner Pike told Liz to go ahead and cook.

"What if we have to run?"

"If we have to run again," Pike said, "this time we'll just leave everything behind."

"What about unsaddling the horses?" McConnell asked.

Pike shrugged and said, "Everybody here can ride bareback, if need be, but I don't really think it'll come to that. Not yet, anyway."

Pike hunched down by the fire with her while she started cooking.

"Still part of the game?" Liz asked.

134

"We're dealing with twice as many Indians now, but I think they're two separate groups—and I think one of them is going to want to work their way around in front of us."

She stared at him and said, "If they do that we'll be cut off."

"Yes, we will."

"What can we do about it?"

"Not much," Pike said. "This is their territory, not ours."

"We could change direction," McConnell said.

They all looked at McConnell, waiting for him to continue.

"Well, since we got here we haven't been traveling up or down, just across the top of the mountain."

"That's right," Whiskey Sam said, "and if we did change direction, they'd expect us to try and get down."

"So," Pike said, taking up where McConnell and Sam left off, "if we go up and they don't find us between them, they'll assume we've gone down."

"And maybe go down after us," McConnell said.

"Leaving us free to get away to a different section of the mountain before we actually do go down."

They all looked at each other, and then Pike smiled and said, "I like it."

They discussed it further over a dinner of beans, bacon and biscuits.

"Of course," Pike said, "we'd have to take care of their point man."

"Point man?" Liz asked.

"The one they've constantly got trailing us so they always know where we are," McConnell said.

135

"How do we do that?" she asked.

"One of us has to go after him," McConnell said.

"Won't they be suspicious when they find him dead?"

"Well, we don't necessarily have to kill him," Whiskey Sam said.

"Why not?" Dick Post asked. "They'll kill us as soon as they get tired of playing this ridiculous game."

"If we kill him they'll think we're trying to hide something," McConnell said.

"Like the fact that we went up the mountain instead of down," Pike added.

"If they find their man unconscious, they might think we're just trying to make a statement," Whiskey Sam said.

"What kind of statement?" Liz asked.

"That we're not afraid of them," Pike said.

"But that would be a lie?"

"Yeah," Pike said, "wouldn't it?"

Later, when they turned in, Liz moved closer to Pike to show she could lie down almost touching him.

"I just need the reassurance that you're here," she said.

"That's all right," he said. "I don't think anybody minds. We've all got other things on our minds."

"Do you think this is going to work, Pike?" she asked. "Do you think we'll really get off this mountain alive?"

"I don't know if this particular ploy is going to

work," he said, honestly, "but yes, I do think we're going to get off the mountain."

"What makes you say that?"

"I have confidence."

"That's all?"

"I'd never forgive myself if I took you up here and got you killed."

"Oh, you can't be responsible for that," she said. "I used my female wiles to get you to take me up here. If I get killed it's nobody's fault but mine."

"I was joking," he said, hurriedly. "No one is going to get killed. You can take my word for it."

"All right, I will."

Several quiet moments passed and then she said, "Did you have the dream last night?"

"No," he admitted.

"Well, that's good, anyway. Maybe that part of your problem is over with."

"Maybe," Pike said, although he was pretty sure he would have traded that problem for the problem with the Indians in a minute.

Chapter Twenty-six

In the morning over breakfast they decided who was going to take care of the Blackfoot point man.

"Pike," McConnell said.

"Pike," Whiskey Sam said.

"Do I have a vote?" Liz asked.

"Yes," Pike told her.

"Pike," she said.

They all looked at Dick Post for his vote and he said, "Why not me?"

"Have you had experience with Indians?" McConnell asked Post.

"Sure."

McConnell looked at Whiskey Sam, who shrugged.

"You're outvoted," McConnell said. "Pike's the only man I know who could sneak up on an Indian."

"That's what I've heard, too," Post said. "Personally, I think I'm better than he is."

Pike looked at Post and something suddenly occurred to him.

"Why do I suddenly get the feeling I know why you

wanted to come on this hunt?'' he asked.

Dick Post turned to face him.

"A man gets tired of hearing how good another man is," Post said.

"Especially when that man thinks that he's as good, eh, Post?''

"Knows," Post said. "I know how good I am. I don't know how good you are."

"Well, I do," McConnell said.

"And so do I," Whiskey Sam said. He was steaming because he realized that he had been used by Dick Post. The man had made a point of befriending Sam, using him to meet Pike. Whiskey Sam wouldn't forgive that.

"I still say I can do it," Post said.

"Then do it," Pike said. "I'm not going to stand here and argue with you about it. Get it done."

The look on Post's face said that he had won a major victory over Pike.

"You know it, too, don't you?" Post said. "You know I'm better than you."

"At what?" Pike asked.

"At everything, at anything."

Pike stared at Post and said, "Do you really think this is the time to go into that?"

Post shrugged.

"As good a time as any, I guess."

"Post—" Whiskey Sam said, but Pike waved him away.

"All right, Post," Pike said. "You want to prove yourself to these people? Go ahead up there and take care of that Indian."

Post frowned. The way Pike was putting it, it

didn't sound right.

"I don't have to prove anything to them."

"Well, are you going or aren't you?" Pike asked impatiently.

Post was confused at this point. Now it would seem that if he did go, he was trying to prove something to the others. If he didn't go then it would look as if he was admitting something he didn't want to admit.

"Pike, why don't you just go and get it done?" Whiskey Sam asked. "Mr. Post don't look like he can make a decision right now."

Pike handed McConnell his rifle and said, "Be back soon. Keep a sharp eye out."

"All right."

Pike looked at Liz and said, "Give me twenty minutes, and then take off your hat."

"What? Why?"

"Just do it," Pike said.

"Okay," she said, frowning. "Twenty minutes."

Pike left them on foot and Whiskey Sam scowled at Dick Post.

"You got some explaining to do, Post," he said, but Dick Post turned away from all of them to pour himself more coffee and give himself time to think.

Pike knew where the brave was. He didn't know if it was the same man who had been watching them all along, but whoever the brave was, Pike always managed to spot him and keep him spotted.

Pike walked away from the fire until he came to a grade. Once he was out of sight of the people at the

141

fire, he assumed he was also out of sight of the Blackfoot brave who was watching them. He started left then, keeping low and intending to work his way to a sharp upward slope so he could get above the brave, but he stopped short when he saw the bear tracks around him. He paused for a moment, looking around, but there was no sign of a grizzly anywhere. Obviously, the bear had been there—but when?

Could he have gotten that close to them during the night without being heard?

Pike had to forget about the bear for the moment and put his mind back on the task at hand. He worked his way to that slope and ascended carefully, not wanting to make any noise or loosen any rocks or stones. Once he got up higher than the Indian was, he'd work his way around him and hope he could get to him before the rest of his hunting party could arrive.

The brave Tall Bear had put on watch was called Wild Feather. Like Tall Bear himself, Wild Feather had eyes for the dark-haired white woman. When he saw the big man walk away he assumed that it was to take care of a call of nature, and he kept his eyes on the three men and the white woman sitting around the fire—especially the white woman. He hoped that after Tall Bear was finished with the woman, that he would turn her over to him. After that, Wild Feather would show his generosity and turn her over to the rest of the braves.

He watched the woman intently, hoping she would take off her hat. Even though her hair was as black as an Indian's, it was wavy instead of straight, and he liked that.

"One more minute," McConnell said to Liz.

They still had not gotten any kind of explanation from Post for his actions, and she was in the process of cleaning up the utensils after breakfast.

"All right, Liz," McConnell said. "It's time. Take off your hat."

Self-consciously she removed her hat, shook out her hair and ran her fingers through it.

As the white woman took off her hat, Wild Feather leaned forward on the stone he was resting on and licked his lips. His tongue was still between his lips when Pike's arm slid beneath his chin and tightened around his neck, cutting off his wind completely.

Wild Feather bit through his tongue and, as the blood ran down his chin, he used both hands to try to remove Pike's arm from his throat. It was no use, though. The Indian was smaller than Pike, and certainly not as strong. After a few moments Pike felt the brave slump in his arm, and then lowered him to the ground.

He checked the brave to make sure he was still alive, then quickly tied the man's hands behind him. That done, he hurried down the slope back to his party, hoping that this was the move that would help them get away clean—and alive.

Chapter Twenty-seven

After Liz took off her hat, McConnell and Whiskey Sam busied themselves getting the horses and mules ready to move. They received no help from Dick Post. In fact, Dick Post seemed to have isolated himself from the others both physically and mentally.

When Pike arrived they were ready to go.

"Are you all right?" Liz asked.

"I'm fine,"he said, touching her hair, "thanks to your beautiful hair.'

She touched her hair, and then asked, "Can I put my hat back on now?"

"If you must."

"I just thought of something," McConnell said.

"What?" Pike asked.

"What are we going to do about the tracks?" McConnell said. "We're gonna leave tracks in the snow that a blind man could follow, let alone a band of Blackfoot Indians."

"You've got a good point," Pike said.

"So what do we do about it?"

"We'll send the mules one way, and the horses another," Pike said.

"You've thought about this?"

"Hey, I had to do something while I was climbing," Pike said.

"Well, that sounds like a fair idea, except do you really think that the Indians can't tell mule tracks from horse tracks?"

"Oh, I'm sure they can."

"Then letting the mules free is not going to buy us much time."

"We're not going to let the mules free."

"We're not?"

"No," Pike said, shaking his head, "we're going to let the horses free."

"The horses?" McConnell said.

"Right."

"And we're going to ride . . ."

"The mules, Skins," Pike said. "We're going to ride the mules."

Very quickly they switched their saddles from the horses to the mules, but not after some argument from a predictable source.

"I'm not giving up my horse," Dick Post said.

Pike, in the act of saddling a mule, looked at Post and said, "That's fine, Post, but if you don't, you're not riding with us."

"What the hell are you talking about?" Dick Post demanded. He looked at all of them and said, "You'd all let him turn me out?"

"A man who'd put his horse above the welfare of

his . . . his friends?" McConnell asked. "What do you think?"

They all turned their backs on Post and finished their preparations to leave. By the time they were done Post had switched his saddle from his horse to a mule.

"What about the supplies?" Whiskey Sam asked.

"We'll just have to take what we can carry. Weigh the last mule down with what's left."

Sam nodded and they doled out the supplies they really needed to survive.

"Now what?" McConnell asked Pike.

"We release the four horses and the remaining mule," Pike said. "Hopefully, it'll take the Indians some time to catch up to them."

"And by that time we'll have had time to get away," Liz said.

"That's what we hope," Pike said.

McConnell walked the horses and mule a way from camp, then slapped a couple of them on the rump and released them.

"You know," Whiskey Sam said, "I had some second thoughts about giving up my horse too until McConnell spoke up. What about you?"

"My philosophy has always been the same, Sam," Pike said. "Never get attached to an animal you might someday have to eat."

Chapter Twenty-eight

When Tall Bear saw Wild Feather, tied up but now conscious, he became disgusted.

"Untie him," he told one of the other braves.

When Wild Feather was free he walked to Tall Bear's horse.

"I am sorry—"

"You let a white man do this to you?"

"He came up from behind me—"

"And you did not hear him?" Tall Bear demanded. He was about to ask another question when Fear Bringer put a large hand on his shoulder.

"Which one was it?" Fear Bringer asked.

"It was the big man," Wild Feather said. "He was very quiet, and very strong."

Fear Bringer looked at Tall Bear and shrugged. He was smiling, though, because more and more the big man was looking like a worthy opponent.

Tall Bear saw that Wild Feather's horse was still nearby so he instructed the brave to mount.

They rode down to where the whites had camped, and dismounted.

"Two sets of tracks," Fear Bringer said.

"They have released their mules to try and throw us off the trail," Tall Bear said.

"A foolish move," Wild Feather said.

Tall Bear gave him a hard stare and said, "You know all about foolish moves, eh?"

Wild Feather fell silent.

"They are beginning to descend," Tall Bear said.

"That means we will not be able to trap them between us and John Kidd's braves," Fear Bringer said.

"Then we must catch up to them and take them," Tall Bear said. "Otherwise they will escape from us and we will be disgraced."

"We will not be disgraced, little brother," Fear Bringer said.

"If we are," Tall Bear said, looking over at Wild Feather, "I will have that fool's head."

"Come," Fear Bringer said, "put aside your anger and let us ride. We will catch them soon enough."

Tall Bear called one of his braves over and instructed him to keep riding on until he found John Kidd and the other braves.

"What shall I tell them, Tall Bear?"

"Tell them where we've gone and that we will meet them back at camp."

The brave nodded and rode off.

"Foolish white men," Tall Bear said, mounting up, "to think that we cannot tell mule tracks from those of horses."

As Tall Bear started to ride in the tracks of the horses, Fear Bringer lagged back and looked at the mule tracks again. Something Tall Bear had said, and the appearance of the mule tracks, did not seem right to him, but ultimately he shrugged and followed the other braves.

150

Chapter Twenty-nine

They camped in the rocks and ate a cold lunch, washing it down with water.

"Do you think they went for it?" McConnell asked.

"I hope so," Pike said, "but let's pick our way north for a while before we start down."

McConnell nodded, then looked over at Post, who was eating away from the rest of them.

"What do you think of him?" he asked Pike.

"Not much," Pike said.

"Seems to want to compete with you awful bad," McConnell said.

"That's just what I don't need right now," Pike said. "If he wants to compete let him come to rendezvous next time." To punctuate his remark he added under his breath, "Asshole!"

"My butt hurts," Liz complained. She stood up and rubbed it with both hands.

"It's these rocks," Pike said. "We'll be down off of here soon."

"Off the rocks," she asked, "or off the mountain?"

Pike grinned and said, "Take your pick."

They came down off the rocks and made camp for dinner. Again, Dick Post sat off by himself when he ate, and made his bed away from them.

"He's doing it to himself," McConnell said. "Nobody told him he can't eat with us."

"Maybe he doesn't like us," Pike said.

"Maybe."

"Maybe he never liked us," Pike said.

"Probably."

"Post!" Pike called out.

"Yeah?"

"You take the first watch!"

Post had already made himself comfortable and cursed beneath his breath as he got to his feet again and picked up his rifle.

"Why'd you do that?" McConnell asked. "I thought I was taking the first watch."

"Ah, to hell with him," Pike said. "I figure I might as well give him reason to dislike me."

"When we get down off this mountain he might decide to do something about that."

"Let him," Pike said. "By then I'll be mad enough to do something about it."

That night Pike had the dream again, only this time the Indians had faces, like the one he had tied up, like the big one.

And for the first time he realized that the bear in his dream was as huge as he remembered, and it was not a case of exaggeration.

In his dream this time he looked around, to see if there was anyone else in the dream besides him, the Indians, the bear, and Liz, who was still lying naked between him and the bear. He thought that maybe he'd see McConnell or Whiskey Sam, but he didn't. There were no other people in the dream.

Another thing he noticed was that everything seemed to be happening in slow motion this time. He felt as if he was running through hip-deep water—in fact, it felt as if everything was happening *under* water.

He reached the point in his dream where he had to decide between the Indians and the bear and waited for a moment, expecting to wake up. When he didn't he was mildly surprised, but didn't let it hold him up any longer. He had to go toward the bear to try to save Liz from it.

Save her for what? For the Indians? If he saved her from the bear and got killed by the bear, then the Indians would have her. What if she preferred to be killed by the bear than captured by the Indians . . . ?

. . . when he woke up he rolled over and shook Liz awake.

"What?" she said, coming awake with a start. "What is it, Pike?"

"Would you rather be eaten by the bear, or caught by the Indians?"

"What?"

"I said—"

"I heard what you said," she said. She sat up and

153

wiped the sleep from her face. It was dark out and she had no idea what time it was. "Did you have the dream?"

"Yes," he said. "Answer the question. Would you rather be eaten by the bear, or caught by the Indians?"

"That's a tough one," she said. "Let me think a moment."

He sat up and rubbed both hands over his face. What the hell was he doing waking her up to ask her a question like that? But then, if he didn't ask her, what would he do when he had the dream again?

"Well?" he asked.

"Uh . . . I think I'd rather be eaten by the bear."

"Why?"

She shrugged.

"At least that way I wouldn't be dying for nothing."

"Why not?"

"After eating me, maybe the bear wouldn't be so hungry anymore."

He stared at her and said, "That's a hell of a way to look at it."

"My mother always said to look on the bright side," she said. "With the Indians, I don't think there would be a bright side, do you?"

He thought a moment about what Indians did to white women most of the time and then said, "No, I guess you're right."

"Can I go back to sleep now?" she asked.

"Sure," he said, "go back to sleep."

"Thank you."

"You're welcome."

He rolled over and went back to sleep and when

McConnell woke him for his watch he realized that he hadn't had the dream again.

He'd have to wait to use Liz's decision about the bear.

"Pike?" Liz said. She was leaning over so none of the others could hear her.

"What?"

They'd decided to risk a pot of weak coffee, just so they wouldn't freeze to death. No bacon, though. That was a scent that could travel for miles.

"Did you wake me up during the night?"

"Yes."

"To ask me a question?"

"Yes."

"Did you ask me . . ." she said, repeating the question he had asked her about being eaten by a bear or being caught by Indians.

"That's what I asked you, all right."

"Why?"

"I wanted to know what to do next time I had my dream."

"I'm in your dream?"

He realized then that he'd never told her that she was in his dream.

"Um," he said, "yes."

"What am I doing?"

"You're naked."

She stared at him and said, "And that's your nightmare?"

"There's more."

"I should hope so."

He described her position in his dream to her.

"Naked," she said, "in the snow?"

"Yes."

"Aren't I cold?"

"I'm sure you are."

"And I'm between you and the bear?"

"Right."

"And there are Indians?"

"Getting ready to shoot at me," he said, nodding.

It was actually doing him good, talking about the dream this way. It made the whole thing seem as silly as hell—and maybe that was her point.

"Well, let me be eaten by the bear."

"That's what you said during the night, when I woke you up."

"Good," she said, "it's nice to hear that I'm smart even when I'm not awake."

"Should we get going?" Whiskey Sam asked, looming over them. "I mean, I'd like to get going before those Indians come back."

"Let's get going," Pike said, standing up.

As Liz emptied out the remains of the coffeepot she said to him, "Pike?"

"Yes."

"Next time you have your dream?"

"Yes?"

"Um, do you think you could give me a blanket, or something?"

"Sure," he said. "What color?"

Chapter Thirty

"Stop!"

Tall Bear turned to see who had called out and saw that it was Fear Bringer.

"What is wrong?" he asked.

"We are going the wrong way," Fear Bringer said, with great certainty. He cursed himself for taking a full day to come to this realization.

"What do you mean?"

"We have been made fools of," he said.

"How?"

"The whites are not riding their horses," Fear Bringer said. "They are riding the mules."

"How can you—"

"I remember now that the mule tracks were deeper than the tracks made by the horses. That means that it was the mules who were being ridden, not the horses. Don't you see? They have us chasing loose horses."

Tall Bear opened his mouth to argue, but then he stopped short. It made sense. On top of what Fear

Bringer had just said, the tracks of the horses had not stopped once to make camp. The whites could not have ridden straight through the night without rest. Even the horses would have needed some rest.

"All right," Tall Bear said, "we will turn back. We will find them before they get off this mountain!"

As they turned and started back up the mountain slope Fear Bringer shook his head in admiration. It was the big man who had fooled them this way, of this he was sure.

Soon, big man, he thought, very soon now.

Chapter Thirty-one

"Whoops!" Whiskey Sam said, stopping his mule.

Pike had seen them at the same time Whiskey Sam had—bear tracks.

"You know," he said, "I think we're dealing with a ghost."

"Oh, yeah?" McConnell said.

"Well, look at how many of this big bruiser's tracks we've seen, and we haven't gotten even a peek at him. If he's so goddamn big, how can he stay out of sight for so long?"

"It's a big mountain," McConnell said.

"It's only so big," Pike said. "We've got to run into him sooner or later."

"He's circling us," Whiskey Sam said.

"What?"

"Every time we've seen his tracks we've been crossing them," Whiskey Sam said. "We're going north and he's going east. Then he turns around and circles us and comes back around again, and we cross his tracks again."

"So you're saying he's stalking us?" McConnell asked.

"Maybe," Whiskey Sam said. "Maybe . . ."

"Let's keep moving," Pike said, "just in case he is. And," he said, raising his voice so even Dick Post could hear him back where he was riding, "let's stay together."

"Maybe we should talk to Post," McConnell said. "He hasn't said two words since you embarrassed him."

"You talk to him, then," Pike said.

McConnell looked at Whiskey Sam, who said, "I don't want no part of him. Pike might have embarrassed him, but he embarrassed me."

McConnell looked back at Post, and then decided to leave him be.

When they stopped for lunch Dick Post rode up on them and said, "I'm not stopping."

"What?" Pike said.

"I'm going on."

"Alone?"

"Why not? You people don't want me here."

"Look, Post," Pike said, "nobody told you to eat alone, sleep alone and ride alone. That's your idea."

"And it's my idea to keep riding while you people sit here, have lunch and wait for the Indians to catch up."

"That mule needs some rest, Post."

"That's another thing," Post said. "I'm tired of riding a mule. I want to get off this animal as soon as possible, and that means I'm gonna keep riding."

"Have it your way, Post," Pike said. "Ride on."

160

"Anyone want to come with me?"

No one replied.

"Have it your own way," Post said. "I'm leaving."

"And good riddance," Whiskey Sam said to the man's retreating back.

They dismounted and started a fire, and Liz put on a pot of weak coffee again.

"Will we be able to make some hot food for dinner?" she asked.

"We'll give it a try, Liz," Pike said.

"Don't do it on my account," she said.

"We'll all need some hot food in our bellies," he said to her.

"Pike?" McConnell said.

"Yep?"

"I'm going to ride back a ways and take a look. If those Indians are closing in on us we'll have to know about it."

"All right," Pike said, "but be careful."

"I will."

"Watch out for Indians," Whiskey Sam said, "and for that grizzly."

"Don't worry," McConnell said. He wheeled his mule about and rode back the way they had come.

Pike smiled at Liz and said, "If McConnell comes back and says he didn't see any Indians, we'll have some hot food for dinner."

"All right," she said.

"Meanwhile," he said, holding out a piece of dried meat to her, "here's your lunch."

"Thanks."

Whiskey Sam came over and sat next to Pike.

"You know, there's something we ain't considered."

"What's that?"

"Well, if I was them Blackfoot I'd've made that second group we saw circle around and get in front of us again, so's they could squeeze us between them. If they did that, we might still run into them."

"Dick Post will run into them first," Pike said.

"That'll be his hard luck."

"Still, by traveling high we might have missed them already."

"I sure hope that's the case," Whiskey Sam said. "I guess this here hunt wasn't such a great idea after all, eh, Pike?"

"The hunt was a fine idea, Sam. It's just the circumstances we can't control."

"You mean like having Post along," Whiskey Sam said.

"That wasn't your fault."

"I feel like a fool letting a tinhorn like that take me in, make me think we was friends when all along he just wanted to use me to get to you."

"He knew we were friends, then."

"I guess so."

"I wonder who told him that."

"We could ask him next time we see him."

"Just between you and me, I wouldn't mind if we never saw him again."

"Coffee?" Liz asked. She was standing over them with the pot and two cups, and they let her pour them each a cup. She took the pot back to the fire.

"Bet you're sorry you brought her along."

"Yeah, I am, but she's been good through it all."

"That she has," Whiskey Sam said. "Solid as a rock. Thinkin' of gettin' married?"

Pike gave Sam a look and said, "Bite your tongue."

162

"Marriage ain't bad, Pike," Whiskey Sam said. "Hell, I been married three times; that's how good it is."

"If any of your wives found you, you wouldn't think it was so good, anymore."

"Ah . . ." Sam said, making a face, "don't even think about that, Pike. I'd rather face those Indians, or even that grizzly."

When McConnell returned he dismounted and accepted a cup of coffee from Liz.

"No sign of Indians," he said after a gulp of the hot liquid. He held the cup in both hands, warming them.

"That's good," Pike said, "but let's get moving, anyway—uh, after you finish your coffee, Skins."

"Thanks."

Pike walked over to where Liz was washing the pot and the cups they'd used, and Whiskey Sam relayed to McConnell what he and Pike had talked about while he was gone.

"Did you see any tracks?" Sam asked McConnell.

"None that had been made by horses," McConnell said, "but I did see something."

"What?"

"Bear tracks."

"The same?"

McConnell nodded.

When Pike came up to them Whiskey Sam said, "Skins saw some bear tracks. That grizzly seems to be wandering about a lot."

"You sound like you'd like to get a look at that grizzly, Sam," McConnell said.

"I would," Whiskey Sam said, "from a distance."

McConnell finished his coffee and shook the residue from the cup.

"I'll stow this in my gear," he told Pike.

"Good, then let's get moving."

They all mounted up and were about to ride on when something happened to stop them.

More than a dozen Indians appeared on a rise ahead of them.

"Looks like we didn't miss them after all," Pike said.

"What do we do?" Liz asked, her voice hushed.

"Don't anybody move," Pike said. "We can't outrun them, not on these mules."

"Then what do we do?" Liz asked.

"We'll have to wait," McConnell said.

"For what?"

"To see what they do," Pike said. "We'll have to wait and see what they do."

"And just . . . sit here?"

"If we run they'll just run us down," Pike explained. He looked at Liz and saw the terror in her eyes. He reached out and put his hand on her arm. "Just don't move, Liz. Not until I tell you to. Okay?"

She looked at him, wet her lips and said, "All right, Pike."

"Pike, look!" Whiskey Sam said.

Pike looked up at where the Indians were and saw what Sam was calling his attention to. The Indians had brought another rider out where they could see him.

"It's Post," Pike said. "They've got Post."

PART FOUR

THE DREAM ENDS

Chapter Thirty-two

"Why haven't they killed him?" Liz asked.

"They're not ready yet," Whiskey Sam said.

"Have they seen us?" she asked.

"Oh, they've seen us," Pike said.

"Then why aren't they moving?"

"Same reason," Whiskey Sam said. "They ain't ready."

"When will they be ready?"

Nobody answered.

"We can't just sit here!"

"She might have a point, Pike," McConnell said. "Somebody has to move first, either us or them."

"If we move first," Pike said, "they might take that as a sign of weakness."

"That's crazy—"

"Pike," McConnell said, "she might have—"

"You're right," Pike said.

"What?" McConnell asked.

"You're both right. Skins, you and Sam take Liz and move over to that stand of boulders. They'll give good cover."

"What about you?" Liz asked.

"I'm going to sit here a spell."

"Why on earth—"

"Come on, Liz," McConnell said. "Pike knows what he's doing."

She looked at the Indians, and then at Pike, and said, "I hope so."

McConnell eased his mule over to the left, followed by Liz, and then Whiskey Sam. Pike kept staring at the Indians, staring at Dick Post. He couldn't tell if Post had been hurt or not. He realized, in fact, that from this distance he couldn't even tell if the man was alive. For all he knew they could have killed him and propped him up on his mule. Yes, that was something else he just noticed, that Post was still on a mule, and not on a horse.

As he watched, five braves separated from the rest. They each had a bow and arrows, with the bows hanging on their backs by the string. They broke away from the rest of the pack and started riding toward him. As they got closer he saw that they had tomahawks in their hands.

As they got closer they suddenly broke into a gallop and, yelling at the top of their lungs, charged toward him, swinging their tomahawks.

He sat stock-still as they reached him, swinging their weapons. They came so close he could feel the breeze, but he refused to flinch or move. That was what they wanted, and he wouldn't give them the satisfaction.

They made several passes by him; then abruptly they stopped and walked their horses slowly back to the rest of their band. When they reached them they simply took up their previous places and Pike waited to see what was going to happen next.

As he watched, they all turned and went back over the rise, taking Dick Post with them.

Pike let out a breath he'd been holding a long time, then turned his mule and rode over to join the others in the rocks.

"My God!" Liz said. She embraced him as he dismounted, and he could feel her shaking.

"Easy," he said, speaking into her hair.

"I thought—"

"It's all right," he said, "for now."

"For now?" she asked, stepping back and looking at him. "What does that mean?"

"It means that they're still in control of the situation, Liz," Pike said.

"Well, we've got to run."

"To where?" he asked. "On these mules we wouldn't have a chance of outrunning them. We gave up that option when we—when I made the decision to take the chance."

"You didn't make the decision, Pike," McConnell said. "We all agreed."

"That's right," Whiskey Sam said. "Ain't no one of us can take the blame for this."

Liz looked at Pike and said, "They're right, you know."

"Sure," he said. He looked past her and McConnell and Whiskey Sam. "We're going to have to sit tight here for a while. We might as well make a fire and have something hot."

"I'll do it," Liz said.

"Thanks," he said.

He collected some kindling, and some of the cow pies they'd picked up along the way—dried cow, horse and mule dung, actually—and she started the fire and got some coffee going. He watched her as she dumped a huge slab of bacon into a pan, filling the air with its scent. After that she made enough beans for an army. It was as if she were trying to make up for all the cold meals they'd had with this one hot one.

It was as if she were preparing for them their very last meal and she wanted to make it the very best that she possibly could.

After they ate they took turns soaking up bacon grease with stale biscuits, one of them always watching for the Indians to return.

"What do you figure?" McConnell asked Pike while Whiskey Sam was on watch.

"I'm going to bring Sam a cup of coffee," Liz said, leaving them.

"I think they'll wait for the others to catch up."

"How long's that going to be?"

"Depends," Pike said. "Depends on how long it took them to discover that we'd fooled them."

"I don't think Indians like being made fools of, do you?" McConnell asked.

"I imagine not."

It was dark and McConnell looked up at the almost starless sky.

"We might think about trying to slip away," he suggested. "It's dark enough."

"On foot maybe," Pike said, "but not with the mules."

"We wouldn't get very far on foot."

"No, we wouldn't."

"So we wait?"

"We wait."

Liz was returning from giving Sam his coffee when suddenly a high-pitched scream of pain cut through the night—and she screamed and clutched at herself, as if she'd been the one who had been hurt.

"What was that?" she asked, her eyes wide with terror. She was holding her own upper arms so tightly she must have been stopping the blood.

"Post," Pike said. "That was Dick Post."

Chapter Thirty-three

They kept the fire going through the night, and kept a pot of coffee on it. When they weren't on watch they tried to sleep, but it wasn't an easy thing to do, not when Dick Post's scream was still echoing through the night—or seemed to be.

Liz sat by the fire, hugging her knees, staring into the flames. McConnell was lying down, trying to sleep. Whiskey Sam was on watch and Pike was watching Liz. The light from the fire was flickering on her face, and he thought she'd never looked more beautiful than at that moment.

"Don't stare into the fire," Pike said.

"Why not?" she asked.

"Look out there," he said.

She lifted her head and looked out at the night.

"What do you see?"

"Black."

"If you hadn't been staring into the flames you'd see something," he said. "Not much, but something."

"What's the point?" she asked.

173

"None, if you're ready to give up."

"What else is there to do?"

"There's always something else to do than die,"
Pike said. "Dying's easy. All you have to do is lie
down and let it happen."

"I see."

"No, you don't," he said, "and that's why I don't
want you staring into the fire."

She looked at him, frowning, and then suddenly
began to laugh.

"You're amazing," she said.

"Why?"

"I'm stiff," she said, "positively numb with fear,
and you're making jokes."

He shrugged.

"Believe me," he said, "it's easier not to make
jokes. Try it sometime and see what an effort it
takes."

"Not for you."

"Oh no? You don't think so?"

"No, I don't."

"Why?"

"Because I think you're the bravest man I've ever
met."

"You haven't known many men, then," he said.
"Not many brave ones, anyway."

"I've known a lot of men," she said. "You forget
where you found me."

"I found you in Clark's store," he reminded her.

"You know what I meant."

"You never belonged there, anyway."

"Oh, no?" she asked. "Do you know where I do
belong, Pike?"

"I don't know," he said. "Maybe in a big house

somewhere back east, or in a big city someplace."

"That sounds nice," she said. "And where do you belong, Pike? Where are you the most comfortable?"

"Out here," he said, looking around. "Right out here where we are now."

"Waiting to die at the hands of some savage?" she asked, frowning.

He shrugged.

"Whatever," he said. "Waiting for an Indian, a bear, a rock to fall on my head. Everybody's got to die sometime. When I do, I want it to be up here."

"You see," she said, "that's what I mean. You're making jokes."

"I'm not," he said. "I'm very serious."

She was about to say something again when suddenly another scream pierced the darkness.

"Jesus," she said, covering her ears as Skins McConnell sat up, "isn't he dead yet?"

"Soon," Pike said, his tone soothing. "He will be very soon."

When morning came Liz fried the rest of the bacon and beans and they ate it. At dinner the night before and breakfast that morning they ate three days' worth of food.

"Maybe we should have saved some," McConnell said when they were done.

"What for?" Liz asked. "So we could last longer?"

"No need," Pike said. "The other braves should be here sometime today. We've still got some dried meat for lunch. I think dinner will be on the Blackfoot."

They took turns again keeping watch, but very

often one of them would join the one on watch, just for the company.

About midday Liz fell asleep. McConnell was on watch, while Whiskey Sam and Pike sat around the fire.

"This is gonna be our last fire," Whiskey Sam said. "Ain't nothing left to burn."

Pike shrugged. He still thought that a move would be made before dark.

"Think we'll get out of this, Pike?" Whiskey Sam asked.

"Don't know, Sam," Pike said. "I sure don't want to look forward to it, though."

"Why not?"

"I don't mind being surprised," Pike said, "but I hate being disappointed."

"You won't have to be," McConnell said from behind him. "Come and take a look."

Pike and Whiskey Sam joined McConnell, and Liz, as if she could sense something was up, woke and joined them.

The Indians were back on the rise to their left, where they'd first seen them, minus Dick Post now, and directly across from them to their right was the other band.

"Looks like the gang's all here and the party's about to start," Pike said.

"How many you figure?" McConnell asked no one in particular.

"Close to thirty," Pike said.

"There's that big buck in front," Whiskey Sam said.

"I see him," Pike said.

"Think he's the leader?" Sam asked.

"I doubt it," McConnell said.

"Why?"

"Biggest one usually isn't the smartest," McConnell said.

Pike paused a moment, then looked at his friend and saw a small smile playing on his lips.

"You're a sick sonofabitch to be making jokes at a time like this."

McConnell looked at him, smiled broadly, and said, "Who's joking?"

Chapter Thirty-four

"It would seem," Tall Bear said, "that they have gone through a lot of trouble for nothing."

"I do not think so," Fear Bringer said.

"Why?" Tall Bear asked, looking at his friend of many years.

"With a little luck, they might have made it," Fear Bringer said.

"Well," Tall Bear said, "their luck has now run out."

"How do you want to do this?" Fear Bringer asked. "Shall we rush them from both sides?"

He knew that John Kidd was watching Tall Bear from across the way, waiting for a signal.

"We will lose some braves that way if we do," Tall Bear said.

"Do you know a way to do this without losing braves?" Fear Bringer asked.

Tall Bear's reply was immediate—so immediate that Fear Bringer knew his friend had been thinking about it for some time now.

"One of us could go and talk to them," Tall Bear said, "and get them to surrender to us."

"Give themselves up for death?" Fear Bringer said. "That is not the way of the whites as I know it."

"We could tell them that we want the woman in return for their freedom."

"That is also not the way of the—"

"It would be interesting," Tall Bear said, "to see how they react."

Fear Bringer fell silent and remained so.

"Would you like me to have John Kidd do it?"

"How would you tell him what you wanted?" Fear Bringer asked. "No, as you suspected, I will go and talk to them. I will talk to their leader."

"The big man."

"Yes," Fear Bringer said, a glint in his eye. The big man suspected that the look in his own eyes was the same look Tall Bear got in his eyes when he spoke of—or thought about—the white woman.

"What shall I promise them?"

"Freedom, in return for the woman."

"Very well," Fear Bringer said, dismounting. "I will tell them."

He started to walk across the snow to the group of rocks where the whites had taken cover. As he approached he saw the barrels of their weapons train on him, but he knew they wouldn't shoot. Not yet, anyway. Not until they heard what he had to say. Not as long as there was a chance for freedom.

Fools.

Chapter Thirty-five

"Here he comes," Whiskey Sam said.

"Which one?" Pike asked. He, McConnell and Liz were sitting with their backs to the stone that Whiskey Sam was leaning on.

"The big one."

Pike gave McConnell a sharp look and the other man said, "That doesn't mean he's their leader, just that he's their spokesman."

"What kind of a deal do you think they're going to offer us?" Whiskey Sam asked.

"Doesn't much matter, does it?" Pike asked.

"What do you mean, it doesn't matter?" Liz asked.

"He means that no matter what deal they offer us, they'll have no intention of keeping it."

"I thought Indians were honorable people."

"They are," Pike said. "Only we made fools out of these. They won't like that."

"He's gettin' within hailing range," Whiskey Sam called out.

"Yeah," Pike said.

He and McConnell started to stand up, and when Liz made a move to follow, Pike put his hand on her shoulder and pushed her back down.

"Stay put."

"I want to see."

"Well, I don't want them to see you."

Pike stood up, standing between McConnell and Whiskey Sam. They all pointed their rifles at the man as he got close enough to talk.

"I want to speak to your leader."

"So speak!" Pike said.

"Who is your leader?"

"We don't have a leader," Pike called back. "We are all equal."

"I want one of you to step out and speak with me," the brave said.

"Jesus," Whiskey Sam said. "Up close he looks even bigger—even bigger than you."

"Maybe it's been his tracks we been seeing, and not a grizzly's," McConnell said.

Pike handed his rifle to McConnell.

"You're going out there?" Liz asked.

"It's the only way," McConnell said.

"I've got him in my sights," Whiskey Sam said. "At the first sign of trouble, he's the first one to get it."

"That makes me feel a lot better," Pike said, and stepped out into the open.

"You are the leader?" the brave asked.

"Yes."

"What is your name?"

182

"Pike."

"I am Fear Bringer."

"I can believe that."

Pike was three feet from the man and could see that he was indeed taller than he was, though he might not have been heavier. He studied Fear Bringer carefully, as if he sensed that soon he'd have to face him hand-to-hand. The Indian was well muscled, but not as thick as Pike through the waist and hips. That meant that Pike had the advantage as far as a center of gravity went, and that was where true strength came from, a good center of gravity.

"You made fools of us," Fear Bringer said.

"That was not our intention."

"What was your intention?"

"To escape."

"And you have not."

"It didn't work," Pike said, with a shrug.

"You accept that?"

"It is a fact," Pike said. "A man would be foolish not to accept what is."

"And now you will die."

"If we must."

"There is another way."

"What is that?"

"The woman."

"What about her?"

"Give her to us."

"I can't do that."

"You speak to the others?"

"Yes."

"And you will not give her to us?"

"I cannot."

183

"If you do not, you will all die."

"We will all go free, or we will all die," Pike said, "together."

"You are foolish," Fear Bringer said, shaking his head. "She is just a woman."

"Then let her go," Pike said. "As a woman she is of little true value to you."

"My friend, Tall Bear, wants her."

"Is he your friend, or your leader?"

"He speaks for our leader," Fear Bringer said, "Strong Wolf."

"Does Tall Bear want the woman for himself, or for Strong Wolf?" Pike asked.

"That does not matter."

"I have heard that Strong Wolf is a man of honor."

"That is true."

"That he is a great man, and a great leader."

"That is true."

"Then take us to him."

"What?" Fear Bringer was not sure that he had heard the white man correctly.

"We will surrender to you if you will take us to Strong Wolf and allow him to decide our fate."

"And you will abide by his decision?" Fear Bringer asked. He had not expected such a suggestion.

"As I said before," Pike said, "a man would be foolish to deny what is."

He could see that the Indian was confused, unsure of how to react.

"I must speak to Tall Bear."

"Speak to him. We await your reply."

Suddenly, it seemed to Fear Bringer that the situation had been reversed on him. It should have been *he* who said that to the white man, Pike.

"I will bring you our reply," Fear Bringer said. He turned and walked away from Pike, and Pike turned and went back behind the rocks.

"Where did that suggestion come from?" Skins McConnell asked.

"It was just an idea," Pike said.

"And a damned good one," Whiskey Sam said. "We'll get more of a fair shake from Strong Wolf than we'd ever get from these bucks."

"That is," Pike said, "if we ever get to Strong Wolf."

Chapter Thirty-six

"Why are they taking so long to decide?" Liz asked nervously.

"Maybe they're arguing about it," Pike said.

"That would be nice," McConnell said. "Maybe we can get them to argue among themselves."

"And forget about us?" Liz asked.

"Not much chance of that," Whiskey Sam said.

"I didn't think so," she said.

"Here he comes," Whiskey Sam said.

Pike and McConnell stood while Liz stayed down. Pike stepped out to meet Fear Bringer.

It had been an argument of sorts that had taken place between Tall Bear and Fear Bringer.

"Why don't you want to take them to Strong Wolf?" Fear Bringer asked.

"Because it is not Strong Wolf who was made a fool of," Tall Bear said.

Fear Bringer smiled and said, "Little brother, that is not the reason."

"It is not? Then what is?"

"You are afraid that when Strong Wolf sees the woman he will want her."

Tall Bear frowned.

"Why do you say that?"

"Because I know you," Fear Bringer said.

Tall Bear hesitated, then said, "All right, we will take them to Strong Wolf."

"If they earn it," Fear Bringer said.

"How will they do that?"

"I will tell you . . ." Fear Bringer said with a satisfied smile.

"What is your decision?" Pike asked Fear Bringer.

"We will take you to Strong Wolf—"

"Good—"

"—if you earn the right."

"And how do we do that?"

"In combat," Fear Bringer said. "One of you will fight one of us. If you win, we will take you to Strong Wolf."

"And if we don't win?"

"We will kill the men and take the woman."

"When would this take place?"

"As soon as we can prepare," Fear Bringer said. "Talk among yourselves about who will fight. I will come for you."

Fear Bringer turned and walked away and Pike backed his way to the rocks.

"Did you hear?" he asked the others.

"We heard,' McConnell said. 'What do you think he has in mind?"

"What do you think, Sam?" Pike asked.

"I think that buck wants to see how good you are,"

Whiskey Sam said. "He's been looking you up and down the whole time you been talking."

"That's what I figure," Pike said.

"What are you going to do?" Liz asked.

"Fight him," Pike said. "It's the only chance we have."

"Which one of you will fight?"

They all looked down at her and Pike said, "Oh, we sort of figured you might like to do it."

She stared up at the three of them for a few moments, then smiled and said, "You guys are sick."

"It's nice that you can smile," Pike said.

"Considering all the alternatives," she said, "it seems the thing to do."

"Pike will fight," McConnell said.

"Why Pike?"

"For obvious reasons," McConnell said.

"I'm too old," Whiskey Sam said.

"And Fear Bringer would crush my bones to powder in a minute," McConnell said. "I'm used to fighting normal-size people."

"Right," Pike said, taking off his jacket and his shirt.

"What are you doing?" Liz asked.

"I don't want anything to restrict my movements," he said, discarding the garments, tossing them down on the snow.

"But it's freezing," she said. "You'll catch your death of cold!"

They all looked at her again and she said sheepishly, "Oh . . . right . . . sorry." She picked up his clothes, wanting to keep them dry.

"Here they come," Whiskey Sam said.

All the braves from Fear Bringer's group were coming across the snow with him. Pike knew that they'd form a circle around the combatants and make sure that neither of them left it until one of them had won—or was dead.

"Are you ready?" Fear Bringer called out.

"I am ready," Pike said.

At that point Fear Bringer stepped aside and a brave moved out from behind him. He was stripped of everything but a loin cloth. He was a big man, though not as big as Pike or Fear Bringer.

"He is called Stone Hands," Fear Bringer said. "He will fight for the Blackfoot."

"That sonofabitch!" Whiskey Sam said under his breath. "He wants to see what you can do first."

"Yeah, it looks that way," Pike said.

"What's wrong?" Liz asked.

"Pike, you want some advice?" McConnell asked.

"I can always use advice," Pike said. Pike was aware of the cold on his bare skin, although it didn't bother him—not yet, anyway. One of the things he liked about living in the mountains was the cold. It made you feel more alive.

Or maybe that was a poor choice of words, considering their present situation.

"If you can, don't give it all you've got," McConnell said. "Don't show him everything. It'll give you an edge when you finally do face the sonofabitch."

"What's going on?" Liz asked anxiously.

"Fear Bringer has another brave fighting Pike," McConnell said.

"Why?"

"So he can watch Pike."

"Can you beat this one?" Liz asked.

"That's what we're about to find out," Pike said, stepping out into the open.

Chapter Thirty-seven

"This is Tall Bear," Fear Bringer said.

Pike looked at the brave who was in charge, the one who was interested in Liz. He was tall and slender, with dark, piercing eyes. Dangerous, but not immediately so. He turned his eyes to the brave he was to fight.

Though not as large as Fear Bringer, the brave called Stone Hands certainly did not seem any less formidable. Looking at his rough hands and large knuckles, Pike could see why he might be called "Stone Hands."

The braves had formed a semi-circle and as Pike stepped into it, they closed it around him and Stone Hands.

"You will fight bare-fisted," Tall Bear said.

"Until when?" Pike asked.

"Until one of you cannot fight anymore," Tall Bear said. "Of course, you know that to Stone Hands, that means until you are dead."

"I kind of figured that."

Tall Bear then stepped right to the rim of the circle of men and said, "Fight!"

Pike regarded Stone Hands critically, waiting for the man to make a move. He hoped to be able to gauge the man's speed and strength before committing himself to a course of action.

They circled each other warily. The one advantage that Pike might have had was that Indians fought more with knives than they did with their bare hands. That Fear Bringer had decided on bare hands was further indication that he wanted to watch Pike carefully, and did not want to take a chance that the big white man would be killed.

They feinted toward each other a couple of times, and then closed in on each other. A roar went up from the others as they grappled with each other, each looking for an advantage. When neither man could find one, they released each other and stepped back.

Pike knew now that he was stronger than the other man. *He* knew that, and no one else did. He could have thrown the man to the ground, but he preferred to break with him, not revealing the fact that his strength was superior.

They circled each other again, and the Indians forming the circle began to shout encouragement to their man.

From behind the rocks, McConnell and Whiskey Sam watched—and Liz managed to stand and watch, as well.

"Nothing's happening," Liz complained, speaking low.

192

"They're sizing each other up," McConnell said.

"What do you think?" Liz asked.

"Pike can take him," Whiskey Sam said. "He just doesn't want to give it away too soon."

"How can you tell?" Liz asked.

"I seen a lot of fights, Liz," Whiskey Sam said. "I know when one man has another man's measure."

McConnell knew it, too. He looked for Fear Bringer in the circle of Indians and found him. The big brave's eyes were glued to Pike, watching every move the big man made carefully, sizing him up. Already, Fear Bringer was looking for an edge, an advantage he could use when the time came for him to face Pike himself.

Fear Bringer looked as if he would be better handled with a lead ball.

Pike grappled with Stone Hands several more times before deciding to finish it. When they closed again he stuck his hip out and pulled Stone Hands over it, slamming him to the ground. As the air rushed from the brave's lungs, paralyzing him, Pike hit him in the face once. One time would have done it, but Pike hit him two more times just for effect, then stood up and stepped away.

Pike saw Fear Bringer and Tall Bear exchange glances, and then two braves stepped forward and helped Stone Hands to his feet.

As the braves began to move away as a group both Tall Bear and Fear Bringer stepped up to Pike, who was for the first time noticing the cold as it dried the perspiration on his bare torso.

"Go back to your people and wait," Tall Bear said. "We will come for you."

"To take us to Strong Wolf?" Pike asked.

"We will come for you," Tall Bear said. He turned and walked away, following the others.

Fear Bringer hesitated, matching stares with Pike for a few moments, then turned and followed Tall Bear.

For a moment Pike couldn't decipher the look the big Indian had been giving him, and then it came to him.

Amusement.

When Pike returned to the others Liz hurriedly handed him his clothes. When he had donned his calico shirt and his jacket she rubbed his torso with her palms, trying to work warmth into him.

"You carried him too long," Whiskey Sam said, critically.

"I know," Pike said. "The big Indian, Fear Bringer, knows, too."

"What will they do now?" Liz asked.

"I don't know," Pike said.

"They're supposed to take us to Strong Wolf."

"Maybe they will," Pike said. "Maybe."

"He could have overpowered Stone Hands any time," Fear Bringer said to Tall Bear.

"I know," Tall Bear said. "He is a smart one."

"And strong," Fear Bringer said. "You will tell Strong Wolf that he is mine."

194

"I will tell him," Tall Bear said, "but who will tell him that the woman is mine?"

Fear Bringer did not have an answer for that.

"Go," Tall Bear said. "Tell them to prepare to leave on their mules, and then call John Kidd in. We will leave as soon as they are ready."

"I will tell them," Fear Bringer said.

Pike had his rifle in his hand when Fear Bringer came back alone.

"Pike!"

"Yes?"

"Mount your mules and prepare to leave."

"All right."

Fear Bringer turned and waved to the braves on the other side, who rode down the rise to join the rest.

"The least they could have done was give us some horses to ride," Liz complained.

"They want to keep us on the mules," Pike said. "That way we won't try to run."

"What's going to happen now?" she asked. "I mean, when we get where we're going."

"Well," Pike said, "I guess that's going to be up to Strong Wolf."

Chapter Thirty-eight

They were ready when the braves rode up to them, and rode their mules out to join them. The braves opened their ranks to let them in, and then closed up around them.

"Not much chance to get away," Liz said, "horses or mules."

"No," Pike said, agreeing.

Tall Bear rode up to them and said to Liz, "You will ride with me."

She looked at Pike immediately.

"She rides with me," Pike said.

Tall Bear seemed to get taller astride his pony and said, "She will ride with me."

"We can do this all day," Pike said, "and it'll come out the same way."

"What way is that?"

"Either she rides with me," Pike said, "or we don't go."

"I could kill you."

"You could," Pike said.

"If you did that," McConnell said, "you'd have to kill us all."

Tall Bear studied all of them for a few moments, then wheeled his pony around and rode to the head of the pack.

"Oh, my God," Liz breathed. "Thank you all."

"Don't mention it," Whiskey Sam said.

After they had ridden a short way Liz said, "Pike?"

"Yes?"

"Why haven't they taken our guns away from us?"

"I guess they don't think we'd be foolish enough to use them."

"Why wouldn't we?"

"Because we're grossly outnumbered. Shooting some of them would only anger the rest of them."

"But . . . they're going to kill us, aren't they?"

"There are two ways to die, Liz," Whiskey Sam said.

"What are they?"

"Quick, and slow," McConnell said.

"Dick Post died slow," Whiskey Sam said, and Liz shivered, remembering the echoing screams of the previous night.

It was almost dark when they finally reached the Blackfoot camp. They were instructed to dismount, and were then led to a teepee by John Kidd.

"You and you," John Kidd said to McConnell and Whiskey Sam, "in here."

"Sure," Whiskey Sam said. "Do we get fed?"

"Inside," John Kidd said.

"After you," Whiskey Sam said to McConnell.

198

"Leave your guns outside."

Sam and McConnell stopped short, then obeyed, leaving their rifles and their Kentucky pistols outside.

"See you later," McConnell said to Pike.

"This way," John Kidd said to Pike and Liz.

"You speak English better than the rest of them," Pike said.

John Kidd looked at him and said, "You mean better than the rest of my people?"

"Oh, yeah, that's what I meant. I, uh, didn't mean to offend you."

"That makes you very different from other white men," John Kidd said.

He stopped them by a teepee that was several teepees away from the one McConnell and Whiskey Sam had entered.

"You go inside, and leave your guns outside," John Kidd said to Pike.

"And what about the woman?"

"She will stay somewhere else."

Liz looked at Pike, so terrified she was unable to speak.

"She will stay here with me," Pike said.

"No—"

"Yes," Pike said.

Kidd and Pike stared at each other, and Pike could see that Kidd was unsure about what to do.

"Check with Tall Bear," Pike said, "or with Strong Wolf." He took Liz's arm and guided her into the teepee, then showed Kidd his guns and very deliberately put them down outside the teepee.

Inside he found enough wood to start a fire to keep

them warm, and then they sat very close together for added warmth.

"What will they do with us?" Liz asked.

"You can ask me that until the cows come home, Liz, and I won't be able to give you a definite answer."

"I know," Liz said. "I'm sorry."

"Don't apologize."

She snuggled closer to him and said, "I wish we could . . ."

"Could what?"

"You know."

"I'm afraid we'd be interrupted."

"I'm hungry, anyway."

"Here," he said, taking some dried meat from his pocket. "I thought we might need this."

"Good thinking," she said, accepting it gratefully.

"I'm sure they'll feed us in a while," he said, taking a bite from his own piece of meat. "They won't want us to die overnight of the cold, or of hunger."

"I'll try to find that comforting."

"Stay here," he said, getting to his feet.

"Where are you going?"

"I just want to look outside."

He moved to the entrance of the tent, peered outside and saw what he thought he would see.

Nothing.

He went back and sat with her.

"What is it?"

"The guns are gone. I guess they don't want us to get any ideas overnight, either."

"I find that less comforting," she said, popping the last piece of meat into her mouth. "Why didn't they take them away from us in the first place?"

"That would have been a sign of weakness," Pike said. "It would have told us that they were afraid of us."

"Maybe it would have shown respect."

"To these people, fear is much more important than respect," he explained.

He looked around, found a blanket and wrapped it around both of them. With the fire, the blanket and each other, they certainly wouldn't freeze to death.

Now he only hoped he was right about the food.

After they were there about an hour a squaw appeared at the tent entrance, carrying food. She put a couple of wooden bowls on the floor and then backed out without saying a word. She did, however, give Pike one long, cow-eyed look before she left.

"I think she was impressed with you," Liz said.

"I'm more impressed with what she brought," he said, picking up one of the bowls and handing it to her before taking the other.

"What is it?" Liz asked, sniffing carefully.

"Who cares?" Pike asked. He picked up a large chunk of meat and popped it into his mouth. It was hot and somewhat gamey, but he was hungry enough that he found it eminently palatable.

He looked at Liz and saw that she was still smelling the meat, wrinkling her nose.

"It's rabbit," he said.

"Oh," she said, and gingerly picked up a piece and put it into her mouth. She chewed thoughtfully, then picked up another larger piece and put it in her mouth.

"How is it?" he asked.

"I've had better, but I don't think I've ever been this hungry before, so it's delicious."

"Right," he said, wondering what she would say if he told her what he really thought it was.

Pike had had rabbit before, and this wasn't it.

He'd tasted dog once, though, and he was pretty sure that's what this was.

Better that she thought it was rabbit.

.

Chapter Thirty-nine

In the morning Tall Bear came for them.

"Strong Wolf will see you," he said, sticking his head into the tent.

They were both wrapped in one blanket, sleeping close together. Pike threw the blanket aside and stood up, then reached down to help Liz to her feet. They stepped outside and found Tall Bear waiting with McConnell and Whiskey Sam. They both had to shield their eyes from the morning sun for a few moments until they became accustomed to the light.

They followed Tall Bear through the camp. Pike looked around. He found it interesting that there were no children and, apparently, only a few women. Obviously this was a temporary camp, subject to moving at any time.

Tall Bear led them to a teepee and said, "Wait out here," and went inside.

"How was your night?" McConnell asked.

"Bearable," Pike said.

"Speaking of which—" McConnell said, but he

was interrupted when Tall Bear came back out.

Pike knew what McConnell had been getting at, and if he'd been able to answer, the answer would have been no, he hadn't had the dream last night.

"Pike," Tall Bear said.

Pike took that to mean that he wanted him to enter the tent.

"What about the others?"

"Strong Wolf will see only Pike," Tall Bear said. "The rest will stay here."

Pike looked at them and shrugged, then bent low and entered the tent.

Seated on the floor was a man who looked to be in his forties, with cheekbones so high and strong that they looked as if they might break through his skin.

"Strong Wolf?"

"Sit," the Indian said.

Pike sat, cross-legged.

"Why did you not try to shoot any of my people?" Strong Wolf wanted to know.

"I wished to get away from them without killing any of them, if possible."

Strong Wolf stared at him. Apparently, the fact that they had not fired at the Indians at all meant something to Strong Wolf. Maybe he was just used to having white men kill his people whenever they got the chance.

"You had two chances to kill one of my braves," Strong Wolf said, "and yet you did not. Was this also your choice?"

"Yes," Pike said. "In both cases there was no need to kill them."

"You value life."

204

"Yes."

"Even an Indian's life?"

"Yes," Pike said. "An Indian is still a man."

Strong Wolf frowned. He was not used to hearing such sentiments from a white man, and he must have been wondering if Pike was telling the truth.

"You are a strange man."

"I do not think so," Pike said. "I have heard that Strong Wolf is wise and honorable. I hope that I can also be described in the same way. No man's life should be thrown away, wasted, whether he be white or red."

Strong Wolf nodded, as if he agreed with the words.

"Tall Bear wants to kill you," he said.

"Tall Bear is neither as wise nor as honorable as Strong Wolf," Pike said. "He is also young."

"Yes, young . . . and headstrong. You know that he was playing with you?"

"Yes," Pike said, "I know he was trying."

"And you made a fool of him."

"Almost," Pike said. "He did catch us, after all."

"He wants your woman."

"I know that."

"Would you be willing to leave here without her?"

"No."

"Is she your woman?"

"She is my friend."

"But not your squaw."

"No."

"Then why would you not leave without her?"

"I would not leave here without any of my friends."

205

"Even if it meant your death?"

"Even then."

"You are honorable, Pike," Strong Wolf said, "and wise."

"I thank Strong Wolf for his kind words."

"I would like to let you leave."

"Obviously I would have to abide by your decision," Pike said.

"In order to take the woman with you, you will have to fight for her. Would you be willing to do that?"

"Fight Tall Bear?"

Strong Wolf shook his head.

"Not Tall Bear," he said. "Fear Bringer."

"But it is Tall Bear who wants the woman."

"And Fear Bringer wants you," Strong Wolf said. "You white people have a saying, something about . . . two stones?"

"Birds," Pike said, knowing what he meant. "Killing two birds with one stone."

"Yes, that is the one," Strong Wolf said, and he smiled. He obviously enjoyed the saying. "Killing two birds with one stone," he repeated.

"What happens if I defeat Fear Bringer?"

"You will go free."

"And my friends."

"They, too."

"And if I don't win?"

"What happens then will not matter to you," Strong Wolf said, "for you will be dead."

Chapter Forty

Once again Pike found himself baring his chest to the elements.

"This one is not going to be as easy as the other," McConnell warned him.

"I know that."

"Don't let him get his arms around you," Whiskey Sam said. "He'll squeeze the life out of you."

Pike nodded at the advice.

Liz came up to him and said, "Pike, are you doing this for me?"

"I'm doing this for all of us, Liz," Pike said. "If I win, Strong Wolf says we can go free."

"Do you believe him?"

"Yes."

"And what about Tall Bear?" she asked. "Will he go along with it?"

"That's another matter," Pike said.

"Are you ready?" Strong Wolf called out to Pike.

"I am."

There were more braves to watch this time, and

consequently the circle they made was much larger. Also, this time McConnell, Whiskey Sam and Liz were part of the circle.

Pike stepped into the circle to face Fear Bringer who, with his black hair long and loose and his finely chiseled muscles, made a magnificent sight. Even Liz's eyes were drawn to him.

Once again weapons were not part of the fight. Fear Bringer obviously enjoyed battling with his hands.

The din caused by the cheering of the braves was deafening, but Pike tried to block it out. He couldn't even hear McConnell, Whiskey Sam and Liz cheering him on. He stared at Fear Bringer, waiting for the huge brave to make the first move. He only hoped that holding back during the fight yesterday would give him some kind of an edge.

Three feet away, Fear Bringer was smiling happily. He sensed that his victory this time would not be an easy one, and that made him happy. Pike was obviously a worthy opponent, and killing him would add to Fear Bringer's legend.

He flexed his large hands, stretched his arms and then advanced slowly on Pike.

The suddenness of it shocked everyone, even Pike. It had never occurred to him that a man of Fear Bringer's size would have such a weak jaw.

Obviously, the large Indian meant to walk up to Pike slowly and grapple with him, eventually managing to close Pike within the circle of his huge

208

arms, but Pike had other ideas.

Having no desire to wrestle with Fear Bringer, Pike waited until the man came within swinging distance and then hit him. He brought the punch from way back and as his hand connected with the other man's jaw he felt as if two of his fingers snapped.

Fear Bringer's head snapped back, a glazed, shocked look on his face. Slowly, blood trickled from his bottom lip, down over his chin, and then he simply toppled over, falling toward Pike, who stepped out of the way. When the big Indian hit the ground face first his nose was smashed flat, and he didn't move.

Then suddenly, it was over, and now everyone was shocked.

"Jesus," Whiskey Sam said.

Pike looked down at the fallen warrior, then turned and looked at Strong Wolf, whose surprise was plain on his face. The Blackfoot leader regained his composure, however, and entered the circle to stand next to Pike.

"Tomorrow, you and your friends may leave," he said. "Tonight, you will eat with us."

"Thank you, Strong Wolf."

Strong Wolf cast a glance down at Fear Bringer, then turned and walked away. Pike turned to find his friends, and came eye-to-eye with Tall Bear, who did not look happy.

He remembered what Liz had asked him, and now he was even more certain that Tall Bear would not easily abide by Strong Wolf's decision.

The look of hatred on the man's face made that obvious.

Chapter Forty-one

Pike sat next to Strong Wolf that night and while they were eating found himself telling the Blackfoot leader about his dream. He didn't know exactly why, or even how it came about, but Strong Wolf had listened very intently, not saying a word until Pike was finished.

"Your dream will come true," he said.

"What?" Pike said. "Why do you say that?"

"It is too strong not to," Strong Wolf said. "It will come true, and you should be prepared for it."

"If it does come true . . . what does that mean?"

"My people would say that you were a shaman," Strong Wolf said, standing up, "a medicine man. That is, if the dream comes true."

"But you say it will."

Strong Wolf looked down at Pike and said, "Maybe it will not. I will see you in the morning, before you leave. There will be ponies for all of you."

"Thank you, Strong Wolf."

Strong Wolf nodded and walked away.

Pike stood up, and suddenly became aware that he was being watched by a few braves. For a moment he couldn't figure out why, but then he realized that they had been sitting close enough to him and Strong Wolf to hear what they had been talking about.

They had heard the words "shaman" and "medicine man."

He felt their eyes on him as he walked away.

The next morning Pike woke, vaguely aware that he'd had the dream again, but he couldn't remember it all. That bothered him.

"What is it?" Liz asked.

"Hmm, oh nothing."

"Did you have the dream?"

"I . . . think so."

"What do you mean, you think so?"

"I just . . . can't remember it all."

"Well, maybe that's good," she said. "Maybe it's fading."

"Yeah, maybe," Pike said. "Come on, let's see if we can't get away from here before Strong Wolf changes his mind."

Strong Wolf was standing with four ponies. The animals were young and strong and it said something about Strong Wolf's opinion of Pike that he was willing to part with such animals. On the ground were the remains of their supplies.

"I would leave here and get off this mountain as soon as possible," Strong Wolf said. "Tall Bear and

Fear Bringer are not in camp, and some of my braves are missing, also."

"I understand," Pike said. "Thank you, Strong Wolf."

Pike helped Liz up onto one of the ponies while McConnell and Whiskey Sam mounted.

"Can you ride bareback?" Pike asked her.

"I'll make it."

"Let's get moving," McConnell said.

"Good idea," Pike said. "Strong Wolf—"

"Go," Strong Wolf said, and turned and walked away.

Chapter Forty-two

When it happened it did so with stunning quickness.

They were riding up a rise and for some reason Liz was in front. As she topped the rise Pike saw the grizzly rise up from behind it, up on its hind legs.

"Jesus Christ!" Whiskey Sam shouted.

The pony Liz was riding reared up on its hind legs and she slid off its bare back and hit the ground. Because they were on a slope, she began to roll back down it, away from the bear.

"That thing's ten feet tall," Whiskey Sam said. He brought his rifle up to his shoulder and sighted down on the bear.

Somehow, Pike didn't think that was a good idea.

"Sam, don't—"

But he was too late.

The sound of the shot echoed loudly and Pike watched the bear. The ball hit him high in the left side, a shoulder shot that didn't do much except anger him. Whiskey Sam had hurried his shot.

"Oh shit—" Skins McConnell said.

The bear came over the rise, headed right for them. McConnell raised his rifle and fired, but as he did so the bear dropped down onto all fours and the shot went over his head.

"Move! Move!" Pike shouted.

The bear began to run down the slope at them, loping along on all fours, blood leaking from its shoulder.

They wheeled their ponies around and began to ride down the slope.

"Split up!" Pike shouted. "Go left, go left!"

McConnell and Whiskey Sam went left and Pike went right, intending to pick up Liz. The bear didn't hesitate, and kept after Pike.

The dream, he thought, the damned dream.

Just at that moment the pony's front left leg snapped as he stepped through the snow into a chuck hole. Pike was pitched over the horse's head and landed on his back, the wind knocked out of him.

The only thing that saved his life was the fact that the grizzly stopped to take a swipe at the writhing horse, tearing open its throat and putting it out of its misery.

Pike rolled over, still gagging for breath, and watched the bear start toward him again. He groped in the snow for his rifle and raised it to his shoulder. He aimed for the bear's head, and when he pulled the trigger all he got was a click.

The rifle wouldn't fire.

The snow must have caused the powder to get wet.

He rose to his feet, his lungs still burning for air, and started to run. Dimly he was aware of Liz calling his name. He only hoped she was running away from him and not toward him.

Now it was as it had been in the dream. He was running through the snow with his useless rifle in his hand. Behind him, he could hear the breathing of the bear. He didn't know where McConnell and Sam were, but they'd have to reload before they could help him.

He was running hard, looking down at the snow, and when he looked up he couldn't believe what he saw.

Tall Bear, Fear Bringer and about six other braves were ahead of him, pointing their bows and arrows at him. In the dream they'd had rifles, hadn't they? He couldn't remember, but the situation was enough to tell him that Strong Wolf had been right.

The dream was coming true!

He turned now to look behind him and wasn't surprised at what he saw. Liz *had* been running toward him and she had taken herself right into the path of the bear, between Pike and the grizzly. Now as he watched she tripped and fell, and was lying in the snow between them, as she had been in the dream.

Indians ahead of him and the bear behind him, but with Liz between him and the bear there was only one thing for him to do.

He was finally going to find out how the damned dream ended.

"Jesus, look," Whiskey Sam shouted to McConnell.

They both wheeled their ponies around and

watched as the bear chased Pike. They also saw Liz run between them and fall.

"Christ," McConnell said. He dropped down to the ground and started to reload his rifle. Seeing this, Whiskey Sam did the same thing.

Would they be in time?

Pike started to run toward Liz, shouting at the bear as he did.

He discarded the useless rifle and took out his Kentucky pistol. In his dream it had also refused to fire, but that might not be the case here. There were enough things different from his dream to give him hope.

As he reached Liz he grabbed ahold of her arm with his free hand.

"Get up!" he shouted.

"My ankle!" she said. "I twisted it."

"Get up, damn it!" he snapped, pulling her to her feet. "Run!"

"Pike—"

"Run, Liz!" he said, pushing her.

As she started to hobble away he turned to face the oncoming rush of a thousand pounds of wounded, angry grizzly.

He heard a shot and heard the ball strike the bear in the side. It did nothing to stop his rush. He heard a second shot and the ball struck the bear low, just above his left hind leg. The animal staggered slightly, but kept coming.

He knew that McConnell and Whiskey Sam had fired to try and help him, but now they were too far away to fire with their pistols, and by the time they reloaded their rifles it would be too late.

It was up to him.

As the bear closed on him it started a sweeping motion with one clawed paw. Pike, moving quickly, stepped inside the swipe. The bear's arm—or leg, Pike wasn't sure what to call it while the animal was standing at full height—struck Pike on the shoulder. The animal's other paw came around and suddenly Pike was trapped in a true bear hug.

The animal lifted him off his feet and he knew that he was just seconds away from being crushed to death.

His arms were outside the grip of the bear, and he realized he still had his Kentucky pistol. Quickly he reached up over his head, jammed the barrel of the pistol beneath the animal's slavering jaw and pulled the trigger, hoping that it would fire.

There was a muffled explosion as the retort of the gun was muffled by the bear's fur. The ball went in under the animal's jaw, drove up through its head into its brain, and then kept right on going out through the skull, taking much of the bear's head and brains with it.

For a moment Pike didn't know what was going to happen. In death throes the animal could still have crushed him, but suddenly the huge bear keeled over backward, with Pike still trapped in its hug.

The bear's fur was rank and warm as Pike struggled to escape from it. In moments McConnell and Whiskey Sam were there, each pulling on one of the animal's huge appendages.

Finally, Pike was loose and rolled free.

"Are you all right?" McConnell asked.

Pike felt as if his ribs had been crushed, but he nodded, taking a moment to catch his breath.

Liz was at his side then, her arms around him.

"I was so scared," she said.

"*You* were scared!" he said.

He took a deep breath and felt the rush of the cold, clean mountain air fill his lungs.

He was alive!

"The Indians!" he said then, looking past Liz.

"Where?" McConnell asked.

"They were there," Pike said, pointing. "Didn't you see them?"

"I didn't see any Indians," McConnell said. "Did you?" he asked Whiskey Sam.

"No."

"Liz?" Pike asked.

"I was too scared to see anything, Pike."

"They were there, I tell you," Pike said, "just like in my dream."

"Then why didn't they shoot?" McConnell asked.

The only thing Pike could think of was that they hadn't killed him because what they saw was his dream coming true, and if Strong Wolf was right, then they suddenly must have thought that Pike was a shaman.

And if they had regarded the huge bear as a god, then they had seen Pike kill a god!

"I don't know," Pike said, "but I'm sure glad they didn't, whatever their reason."

EPILOGUE

Using the three remaining Indian ponies, they made their way to Remsen's Crossing, a settlement just slightly larger than Clark's Fork. It even had a doctor, who checked on both Liz's ankle and Pike's ribs. With nothing broken, they separated, looking for their choice of food, drink, or bath.

After Pike had soaked in hot water for a while he went over to the settlement restaurant, where he met Liz out front.

"Hungry?" he asked her.

Also fresh from a bath, she said, "I'm starved."

They found McConnell and Whiskey Sam having a meal.

"Buffalo steak," Whiskey Sam said, smiling. "Figured if I couldn't catch one one way, I'd catch it another."

"Sounds like a good idea," Pike said, and he ordered one, also, and a drink. Liz went along with the rest of them and ordered the same thing.

"There's a hotel down the block," McConnell said

to Pike. "It ain't much, but I thought I'd take me a room tonight and leave you the tent."

"I appreciate that, Skins," Pike said, looking at Liz, who smiled at him.

After dinner McConnell and Whiskey Sam went off to find amusement for themselves, and Pike and Liz went back to the tent—to say goodbye.

"Where will you go?" Pike asked.

They were lying together on a blanket, having just made love for the first time since Clark's Fork.

"Probably east," she said. "I think I've had enough of this life, for a while."

"Can't say I blame you," he said.

"Of course," she said, "I'll have to borrow some money from you—but I'll see that you get it back."

"Well, considering your former profession," he said, sliding his hand down to cup one of her buttocks, "maybe we can make a deal."

"Maybe we can," she said. She slid her hand down and wrapped it around his semi-erect penis. Soon she had him standing at full mast, and leaned over him to take him into her mouth.

She sucked him eagerly, making considerably more noise than she had when they were on the mountain that night. She slurped and sucked until he was ready to come, and then he pulled her away and up on top of him. She lifted her hips and he slid into her easily, gasping at the heat of her. She began to ride him then, coming down on him hard each time, and the fact that he was lying on the hard ground made for maximum penetration each time she did.

222

Finally, she came down on him, gasped, and stayed down, grinding herself into him. She bit her lip as her orgasm overtook her, and then he bellowed out loud when he exploded into her . . .

"Think you got your money's worth?" she asked in his ear.

"Woman," he said, "you probably earned enough to take you around the goddamned world—twice!"

"Well," McConnell said, the next morning over breakfast.

"Well what?" Pike asked.

"Did you have the dream last night?"

"I don't think I dreamed at all last night," Pike said.

"I guess it's gone, then."

"I won't know for sure for a few nights," Pike said, "but I think you're right."

In fact he felt more relaxed than he had in weeks, because he truly felt that what had happened on the mountain had successfully done away with the dream for good.

"Think Strong Wolf was right?" Whiskey Sam asked.

"About what?"

"About you being some kind of magic man?"

"There's nothing magic about me, Sam."

"Then how do you explain that dream coming true?"

"I don't," Pike said. "All I want to do is forget it."

"Sounds like a fine idea," McConnell said, forking a piece of ham into his mouth.

223

"Besides, the dream didn't come true . . . exactly."

"What do you mean?"

"Well, for one thing," Pike reminded them, "in my dream Liz was naked."

Whiskey Sam looked at McConnell with a grin on his face and McConnell said, "Well now, that was our loss, wasn't it?"